For Libbi and Charles, with love and gratitude; and for Trudy, who is always waiting when I return from the land of make-believe.

Chapter One

Ames Colville hated seeing the bottom of the barrel. Any barrel.

As a boy he had hated Sunday nights. Last of the weekend. As a man he still did, even though his schedule was his own. The end of a good book made him blue. He resented low tide, and the struggle for the last bit of toothpaste in the tube. He resented ticking clocks, because they made the sound of time running out.

Thus he had observed his 70th birthday with a marked lack of enthusiasm. And after his doctor said the word "biopsy," he went home and threw a lamp across a room.

Walks beside the sea were his balm. And so it came about that on a bright October afternoon he stooped to fetch a razor clam shell and held it high.

"When I was a kid, we called these Chinese fingernails," he said.

"Me too," Peter Llewellyn said. "I wonder what Chinese kids call them."

"Huh," Colville said.

He threw the shell aside, and they walked on. The breeze lathering the surf had a bit of autumn nip. The sun -- already slipping toward its appointed lower place in the winter sky -- threw long shadows behind them. At their approach, a flock of plovers burst upward from water's edge.

"Migrating now," Colville said.

"Expect so."

"Winter is a dead time. The sun goes south. The tourists leave. Even the birds have sense enough to go somewhere else."

"It's the natural cycle."

"Doesn't mean I have to like it. Drab is drab."

They walked on in silence. Atop a distant piling, a cormorant spread its wings to dry in the sun. Nearer ahead of them, a sand crab scuttled into its hole.

"Amazing things," Colville said, gesturing at the crab hole. "They have gills and air sacs, too. They can hold oxygen in the air sacs for weeks."

"All of coastal life is a wonder if you ask me," Llewellyn said. "And speaking of asking me, what's on your mind, Ames? It's not like you to beat around the bush."

Colville slowed, touched the knuckle of a forefinger to his lips.

"Cancer. Maybe."

"Oh. Sorry. I'm very sorry. When will you know for sure?"

"A week. Maybe ten days."

"What kind?"

"Throat."

"They have pretty good outcomes with some of those nowadays."

"And pretty bad outcomes with others."

Llewellyn paused and turned his face to the sun.

"So, you've finally decided you need to talk to a clergyman."

"Maybe I just wanted to talk to a friend."

"I'm a priest, Ames. Don't expect me to act like I'm not."

"You know that I have a hard time with some of that, Pete. A lot of bad gets done in the name of religion."

"A lot of good gets done, too."

"I know. But I still have a hard time with it."

Llewellyn turned and studied the long trail of their footprints in the sand.

"OK," he said at length. "I hear you. so how can I help?"

Colville gestured away from the sea.

"The patio bar at the Island Club is open. Let's go talk about this over a snort."

They climbed to a wooden catwalk over the dunes and thumped toward the restaurant's glass front wall. A gazebo marked the halfway point. When they reached it, Colville stopped and turned to scan the scene.

"I never get tired of it," he said. "I was born and reared here, and I never get tired of it. I love the smell. It's the smell of life. And the motion. The ocean is never still. Even in the wintertime, when the rest of the world looks dead, the ocean is alive and moving. And at night? If there are no clouds? Sometimes I come out here and I stand as still as I can and look up. And I think, 'I don't have words for that. No one has words for that'."

Llewellyn flashed a grin and took him by the arm.

"Careful Ames. Next you'll be talking about God, and I know you wouldn't want to do that."

Colville muttered "smartass," and followed a chuckling Llewellyn to an outdoor bar with a fake thatched roof. The barkeep was a handsome blonde woman flirting with middle age.

"What'll it be, boys?"

"Maker's Mark?" Colville said, cocking a look at Llewellyn.

"Yes," Llewellyn said. "And make mine a double. My friend is questioning my vocation today."

Colville pulled a mock grimace.

"Am I that difficult?"

"Only when you're awake. But that's a conversation for another time. How can I help you?"

Colville took a long moment. Then he spoke almost as if to himself.

"Contrary to what people think, old folks are pretty much like everybody else. We're just a little quicker to get tired and cranky. Otherwise, we really are a lot like everybody else. The end of things is out of sight. Even when you get to be my age, you tell yourself you could have 20 more years, and 20 years is a long time -- too long to see it all clearly. The end is beyond the horizon. But then, when you get a possible diagnosis, the far side of your life has parameters. Limits you can put numbers on. Numbers you can get your mind around. And you begin to think in a new way about how to use whatever time you may have left."

"And you are thinking about …?"

"Retirement. Wouldn't be all that much of a step, actually. Lew's already doing most of the heavy lifting at The Sand Dollar."

"Would you want him to take over?"

"Yes, if he'll stay."

"But you're not sure he would."

"No. And that's one place where I may need your help. You know him. You're close to him."

"You mean you want me to persuade him to stay?"

"No. I want you to help us figure out what's best for him, and for the paper."

"And for you."

"Yes. I want to be sure I use my final years well. To be intentional about it. There may be a lot of them, there may be only a few. But I want to focus my thinking about them. I've spent my life meeting expectations and schedules. My own and other people's. I've come out on the lucky end of things. I have means. I have my health -- so far. I can do pretty much whatever I please. But I'm not sure what that is. You know, a lot of guys get to be my age, and they've spent so much of their lives on the treadmill that they're not even totally sure who they are. Maybe I'm one of those, too."

"Maybe. So, for starters, tell me how things stand with Lew."

"He's a good young man, Pete. You know that."

"Yes, I do."

"And he's got talent. He's one of the best. He could take over The Sand Dollar and make it even better. He could be a fine newspaper editor for Yaupon Bay."

"But …?"

"A part of him still yearns to go for the big time. For the metropolitan dailies and the big stories."

"You were in the big time. Your civil rights reporting made a difference.   The big time isn't necessarily the wrong goal for a young fellow like Lew. And he has a natural re-entry into the dailies. He could go back to that development program with Pole Star. Back to The Advocate. Hell, Ames, your family sold The Advocate to Pole Star. They must have thought it was an OK company."

"Yes. All that's true."

Llewellyn signaled for a bowl of bar nuts. He turned on his stool to face Colville.

"I hear that 'But' in your voice again."

"The dailies are changing, Pete. The Advocate is changing, and it will keep on changing. Newspapers are under so much economic pressure to keep their vigor, even to survive. They are more and more driven by calculations of what the public will be willing to buy. That's not journalism, Pete, that's merchandising. And daily newspaper editors are becoming merchandising managers."

"They still have a lot of influence. He could make a difference. You did."

"Yes. I made a difference. But I didn't make the biggest difference. I broke the eggs. Other people had to make the omelet, if one was going to be made. After the cameras and the hotshots like me left town, ordinary citizens had to work and struggle together to make their communities *be* communities in a new way. Citizens, Pete. Citizens. That's what The Advocate will gradually cease to be. A citizen of this community."

"And The Sand Dollar could fill that vacancy? Even as a weekly?"

"I like to think it already has, and that it can continue. Frequency isn't crucial. Substance, tone, texture -- a sense of understanding and citizenship. Those matter. The Advocate will have power, yes, even when it becomes just one more commodity for sale. But The Sand Dollar can be a voice of leadership."

"Which would be good for Yaupon Bay, but not necessarily for Lew."

"Exactly. I love him like a son, Pete. I wouldn't want him to stay here out of a misguided sense of duty. But I wouldn't want him chasing false dreams, either. The future he imagines may cease to exist."

"So, he doesn't know about the cancer thing?"

"No. It may be a false alarm. I don't want it affecting his thinking."

"But of course it would affect his thinking. And it should. If he decided to stay, he'd be presuming you'd still be in the picture somehow. If he decided to go, he'd be presuming you'd carry on with the Sand Dollar. But you might not be able to carry on. He's entitled to know that, Ames. It wouldn't be right to spring it on him after he's made an uninformed decision."

"Well, I'll have to think about that. Meantime, I want to ask you to help me. Help both of us."

"And so you want me to …."

"Put out some extra antennae when you're around us. Counsel us. You're our friend. You know both of us. Help Lew see the right factors to weigh in his decision. Help me figure out what to say to him about it -- or whether to say anything at all."

"And all the while, you want me to help you conceal from our mutual friend what may be the biggest factor he should weigh."

Colville pinched the bridge of his nose and looked down at the surface of the bar. "Maybe not," he said. "I promise you I'll think that through again."

Llewellyn put a hand on his forearm.

"Look, Ames," he said. "Just for your own sake. About you and me and the cancer business. Now, really."

Colville flicked an impatient gesture.

"If the diagnosis is bad, Ames, you could be dealing with some tough thoughts. Thoughts you've never had before."

"We'll have some talks, I'm sure. But I just don't think I'm going to want you trying to save my soul."

"OK, OK. I hear you. For now, at least, I hear you."

"So, you won't try?"

"I don't promise that. I just promise that I won't let you see me trying."

Colville eyed him for a long moment, then broke into a rumbling laugh.

"You know, Pete, if the priests' union ever gets wind of the real you, they'll drum you out."

"I hope not. I need the work."

Colville flinched at the sound of a cell phone ringtone. He fumbled inside a jacket pocket.

"Mine," he said. "I hate the damn things. But nowadays you can't do without them. Hello? Yes, Lew. Just having a drink. What's up?"

The answer went on for a time. Colville's face fell as he listened.

"OK. Thanks for letting me know. I'll be in soon."

He darkened his phone and turned to Llewellyn.

"Grace Baptist Church has burned. It's arson."

"How do they know already that it's arson?"

"Gasoline everywhere. And Channel Nine got a note claiming responsibility."

"What did it say?"

" 'I did the black church. Before I'm through I'll do a place with people in it.' He signed himself Omega."

"Omega," Llewellyn murmured. "The End. Oh, no."

Chapter Two

        Billy Wakefield knew that he was a darn lucky kid.
Sometimes the happy idea of it filled him so full he just had to say it
out loud.

        Billy Wakefield, you are one darn lucky kid.

        He figured it was OK for him to say "darn," because he had
pretended once to let it slip out where Mom could hear, and she
hadn't scolded him or corrected him or anything -- just grinned a
little grin and kept on stacking the dishes.

        He knew there were other kinds of words. The kind that Dad
really did let slip out sometimes, and Mom would frown and say
"Bill," real low and kind of serious, and Dad would look down and
then up at her, like he knew that officially he had done something
wrong only he really didn't think it was so bad, and she would shake
her head just a little only she was also kind of smiling.

        To say those kinds of words, Billy figured, you had to be
grown up -- or at least closer to it than he was in the third grade.
One day, when the time was right, he was going to ask Dad how old
you had to be to say those words. Just so he'd know.

        That was one of the great things about Dad. Mom too, for
that matter. You could ask them just about anything, and they would
stop whatever they were doing and sit down with you all polite and
serious and talk to you straight on until you told them yes, you had
the answer. They wouldn't shush you or wave you off like you didn't
matter because you were only a kid. They would really talk to you.

        Another great thing about Mom and Dad was that they didn't
fight. For sure they didn't fight like Sammy Winthrop's Mom and
Dad, who would do it right in front of you like you weren't even really
there or something. Their faces would get all dark and they would
get all loud and nasty. You almost thought they wanted to hurt each
other.

        Sometimes it looked like they almost thought it, too, because
they would stop all of a sudden, like somebody had jerked them
away by the back of their collars. And they would get real quiet and
not say "sorry" or anything, but you could see they were wishing

they hadn't said some of what they said. And they would just go to separate rooms and then later go on with their day, kind of quiet still, but not fighting any more.

It bothered Sammy. You could tell, even though he didn't talk about it much -- only sometimes, when it happened right in front of you, and ignoring it would be kind of like pretending you didn't hear a great big thunderstorm. When his Mom and Dad had gone their way to be quiet, Sammy would say something like, *It's not a big deal. It's just something grownups do.* And because he liked Sammy, Billy didn't answer that he thought some grownups did some things they shouldn't, and scaring the dickens out of their own kids would be way up near the top of the list.

Billy's Mom and Dad didn't fight, but they did get serious with each other sometimes. You could tell by the way their voices changed, and by the look on their faces. They weren't mad, they were just talking about stuff that really mattered, so they were being extra careful.

A lot of times it was because Mom got all filled up with being anxious about Dad's job, and she had to let it out, and Dad knew he had to listen and deal with it and help her through it. Billy thought it was way cool to have a dad who was a firefighter, but Mom worried a lot that the job was dangerous and that he would get hurt.

She would say something like, *Bill I worry so much when you're on a shift. Every time the phone rings I jump because I'm afraid it's someone calling to tell me you've been burned or injured or something. I worry so much.*

And he would say something like, *Muffin, I'm so sorry you're afraid, but we are very carefully trained and very carefully supervised. I'm probably safer on a call than I am on the Interstate. And it's what I do, love. It's what I do.*

Her real name was Sarah Jane but Dad always called her "Muffin." He used it like it was a word they had between them and it belonged to them and nobody else.

And they would go on in that way, back and forth, serious but gentle, until it looked like she had got it all out of her one more time, and he had helped her one more time, and they would go back to everyday stuff until it happened again.

Billy had never figured out what Dad meant when he said, *It's what I do, all* low and slow and super serious. It seemed to be one of things that grownups say and grownups understand, and you probably had to wait until you were a grownup before you would get it and care about it.

But he'd been saying it more than usual lately, when he and Mom got serious with each other about the church-burning thing.

Billy didn't understand why anybody would want to burn a church. He didn't understand, because deep down inside, where he kept the stuff that he didn't want even his friends to know, he pretty much liked church. Theirs had a sign with a cool red, white and blue shield on it, and a word that was a little too long for Billy to handle the first time he tried to read it. Mom said the world was "Episcopal," and that it meant their church had bishops, and they were kind of like the ministers' bosses. Billy wondered why the sign didn't just say "bishops" or even "bosses," but then he figured maybe it was another one of those things you had to be a grownup to care about.

Billy thought Father Pete was a pretty cool minister. For one thing, he had a lot of muscles. Dad said he had been a boxer -- a kind of a fighter -- when he was in the Navy. Father Pete was super friendly and liked to have fun and never was stuffy or anything. He didn't even mind when people called the church "Jimmy's." The official name was "St. James By The Sea," Billy knew, but a lot of folks just called it "Jimmy's" and said it like it was a real loving thing.

One of the things Billy really liked about Father Pete was that he believed in short sermons. He liked to say, *If you can't say it in ten minutes you' haven't thought it through yet.*

Father Pete's sermons were a lot better than the ones where Sammy's family went to church. Billy had gone there with them once after a sleepover. Billy thought their minister would never finish. He went on and on like nobody had anything else to do that day but listen to him. He went on so long that Billy finally had to pee, and completely lost track of what the minister was saying because he had to pee so bad that he pretty much had to concentrate on not wetting his pants.

He had worried about not paying proper attention and finally confessed to Mom about it. She had been great, just like she always was. She listened until he finished explaining and then hugged him and told him not to worry, that you really don't get in trouble with God for needing to pee during the sermon. He felt better after that, but he did promise himself that he wasn't going to go back to Sammy's church if he could help it.

Since the church burning thing was a mystery to him, he listened extra hard when Mom and Dad talked about it, so maybe he could understand it. Also, he tried to read some of the articles in the newspapers that they left on the coffee table in the living room.

The articles were hard for a third-grader, but he thought maybe he got the sense of them. The church was one where mostly black people went. It had been around for a long time, and it was a big deal because people from there did stuff in something called the civil rights movement.

When Billy asked them what that was, they got real serious for sure. The both sat down with him. They explained that years ago black people had been treated in a lot of ways that were very wrong and unfair. They said that black people organized, and got together with white people who felt the same way, and began working to get things changed.

And it got to be kind of like a great big argument, because some other people didn't want to see things changed. There were marches in the streets, and big fights in the government. And some very bad things got done. Some people got hurt. Some people even got killed. And some churches where black people went got blown up or burned down.

But the people who thought unfairness was wrong stuck to their guns, and eventually things did change, and new laws got passed, and things began to get better. And Mom and Dad explained to him that this was a good thing, because nobody should be treated badly just because they are a different color.

Billy certainly agreed with that. And he could see that Mom and Dad were extra sad about this new church-burning thing because they had thought that kind of bad stuff was over and behind now. They were extra sad and afraid to see that maybe it was going to start happening again.

Mom was extra sad for another reason, too. She was afraid if that kind of church-burning stuff got started up again, it would make Dad's job more dangerous. He had heard them having one of their talks about it.

Bill, arson fires are extra dangerous, aren't they? Because of the accelerants. Because you don't know going in what the arsonist has set up. Aren't they? Admit it. Look what happened to Toby.

Yes. They are more dangerous. But Toby took a reckless risk. He violated procedure.

Bill, he thought he heard people inside the church, and he went in for them. And you would have done the same. And you will, if it happens again. This guy is going to do it again. He has said right out that he's going to do it again.

Yes. He has.

Oh, Bill. I'll die if you get hurt or worse. And Billy will lose his world. He adores you. And Ivy. What about our little Ivy? She's just a tot.

It's even more than just a job now, Muffin. With a guy like this on the loose, it's even more than just a job for me. And all of us need to stand up against this kind of thing in whatever way we can. You and I have black friends. Those people whose church got destroyed? They are citizens of our town. We have to stand up. All of us. And now I have to do this. Especially now.

Mom had said *Yes, I know,* with a kind of sadness in her voice, like she wanted to cry but didn't think she should.

And so, the church burning thing made Billy sad, too. He didn't like it when Uncle Toby got hurt, even if he wasn't really an uncle, just a family friend. He was a pretty neat guy, and paid a lot of attention to Billy, and had a super cool train set that was so big it filled up one whole room of his house. Uncle Toby's wife Aunt Inez said they didn't need kids because Toby was one himself and that was enough. Sometimes Aunt Inez didn't talk very nice about Uncle Toby.

He didn't get hurt super bad, and he was getting better already, so all that was kind of over and getting to be OK. But Billy didn't like thinking about that thing Mom had said about Dad: *Oh Bill, I'll die if you get hurt or worse. And Billy will lose his world.*

Billy knew what Mom meant by *or worse,* and boy oh boy was she right about that. Billy didn't know what he would do if something really bad happened to his Dad.

He could hardly stand even to think about it.

Chapter Three

        Tip the bartender -- wiry, black-clad and bald as an egg --
appeared at tableside and   nodded hello.
        "Lew. Father Pete. Just the two of you?"
        "No," Lew Perry said. "Ames will be along. He got held up.
Phone call."
        "Want to go ahead with your drinks? Bartender's choice
today. All Carolina products. You tell me if you want beer, hard stuff
or wine. I'll decide the rest."
        "Beer," Lew Perry said.
        "Hard stuff," Peter Llewellyn said. "But nothing fancy."
        Tip disappeared through the crowd milling in the bar of
Saltmarsh Lilly Randolph's Seafood Castle. Best seafood between
Washington and Atlanta, according to Lil, who liked to add that it
ain't braggin' if it's true.
        "You said Ames got a call?" Llewellyn said.
        "Yes. From Hood. About the church burning."
        "I guess he and Larkin and Aimee would be all over that.
Ames, too. It takes him back to some of the bad old days."
        "They were good for his career. And he accomplished good
for a lot of people."
        "Yes he did. But he had to watch a lot of outrage. And
suffering. They were hard times for anybody with a social
conscience. Especially hard if you were an eyewitness up close."
        "Before my time, mostly," Lew Perry said. "It showed how
much good journalism can matter. Ames showed how much good
journalism can matter."
        "Yes, he did. How long have you been with him now? A
couple of years?"
        "Two and a half."
        "You only promised one, as I recall."
        "Only one. But I've been learning a lot."
        Llewellyn lounged into the corner of the booth and stretched
his legs along his seat.
        "What are you working on? At the paper."

"The usual day-to-day stuff. And a real estate thing."

"Real estate?"

"Yes. It looks like somebody's buying land sort of on the quiet, piece by piece. Up north of town, past the beach strip. Just south of where The Barren begins to close in on The Highway. Between town and there. A piece here, a piece there. Lots of time in between the buys. But all in that general area. The deals are being fronted through a Charlotte law firm."

"How did you find out about it?"

"Tip from a source in the courthouse."

"Have you asked the law firm what they're up to?"

"Not yet. I don't really know what I'm asking about, except that they are buying land. Right now they could just tell me it's private and to go away. I have to dig a little, get enough to push back when they try to stonewall."

Tip re-emerged and put down drinks.

"Red Oak lager," he said to Lew. "Brewery's near Greensboro. Father Pete, I've seen you take a martini. This one's made with Cardinal gin. Distillery's in King's Mountain. Up near Charlotte."

The two of them sipped and nodded.

"I should let you choose my drinks more often," Llewellyn said. He surveyed the busy room. "Lil's is jumping this afternoon."

"Friday happy hour, "Tip said. "All the yuppies are cranking up for the weekend. Got to spend some of that money. Rates these kids get paid, they have to work at getting rid of it." He flashed a grin. "And I'm glad to help them out. Excuse me, guys. Have to get to it."

Llewellyn sipped again, held his drink up to the light, settled back into his corner.

"You like the work? At The Sand Dollar?"

"Yes, I do. And Ames is a great teacher."

"You gonna stay?"

Lew eased out a long breath. "I don't know."

"How will you decide?"

"I don't know. It's tough. I didn't expect it to be so tough to decide."

"Well, OK, taking it step by step, why might you decide to leave? Do you want to make a lot of money? Or to be famous?"

"No. None of that."

"Do you know what you want?"

"Yes, I think so."

"And it is …?"

"I want to matter."

Llewellyn wheeled forward in his seat and laid his forearms on the laminate tabletop.

"OK. You want to matter. Let me ask you the sixty-four-dollar question: To whom?"

Lew furrowed his brow. "I don't understand."

"You want to matter. To whom? To whom do you want to matter?"

"Well, just in general, I want my life to amount to something that's important."

"To whom?"

"Come on, Father Pete. You're playing word games with me."

"No, I'm not. I'm trying to suggest that your life's work first has to matter to you. Be important to you, before it's important to others. So, let's consider a couple of scenarios. Suppose you go back to the dailies and work your butt off but you just don't make it to the big time. That happens, you know. Lots of talented people out there competing for the brass ring. Would you matter then? Or suppose you make it to the big time and it isn't what you thought it would be. Suppose you just don't like it. The industry is changing, even at the top. Would you matter then? Have you thought about any of this?"

Ames Colville pushed his bulk through the crowd and slipped into the booth beside Lew Perry. Tip, following in his wake, put a glass of whiskey in front of him.

"Ah," Ames Colville said. "Right on time with my Maker's Mark."

"Nope," Tip said. "Not Maker's Mark. Bartender's choice today. That's Rua. American single malt. Distilled in Charlotte. Try it. It's good stuff."

He wheeled away without waiting for reply. Colville took a tentative sip.

"Well, I'll be darned. It really is quite good."

He took a deeper sip.

"You two look serious. Solving the world's problems?"

"Not exactly. Father Pete was just busting my chops. How was your phone call with Hood?"

"Somber. The church burning has touched a nerve with them. They're going after it full bore."

"It's touched a nerve with me," Peter Llewellyn muttered, "and I'm not black."

With a plump forefinger, Colville slid his whiskey glass from side to side. "Hood wants me to help them," he said.

"How?" Lew said. "With what?"

"A guy has disappeared off the federal radar screen. The federal people are worried that he's gone underground for some reason. Hood, too. He and his folks want to find him. They want me to help."

"What guy?"

"The federal people nicknamed him The Gandy Dancer. He's a white supremacist. Also, a savant of sorts. Very articulate, very well read. The nickname comes from railroad work. He hired out for track maintenance. Moved around the region that way. Always preaching hate. Always nearby when trouble broke out."

"Ever prosecuted?" Lew said.

"No. He's never been caught with his hands directly in anything illegal. But the authorities have him marked as a serious agitator."

"So he disappeared a while back?" Lew said.

"Yes."

"Why is Hood focused on him?"

"Because he was last seen at a rally near here."

"How do Hood and his people know the feds have lost him?" Llewellyn said.

"Aimee hacks into their computers on a regular basis."

"Should have known."

"And Hood wants you to help them locate this guy?" Lew said. "He thinks you can do things that he and the feds can't?"

Colville looked down at the tabletop. "I have sources," he said. "From the old days."

Lew raised a puzzled eyebrow.

"You have sources who could lead you to a guy like that?" he said. "Why would those kinds of people talk to you?"

"What kinds of people?" Colville said.

"The kind who would know him or any details about him, much less have access to him."

A shadow crossed behind Colville's eyes, and his face took on a hard cast. He took a long pull on his whiskey.

"Fear is why. Fear. When something like this church burning thing got loose in a community, everyone was afraid. The victims -- the targets -- were afraid, sure. But they didn't just take it lying down. They didn't just sit around waiting for the next outrage. They took steps to protect themselves. They developed early warning networks, sources of information. They talked to people who talked to people who talked to people," he said. "Bits of information got around. Even gossip could be helpful. Straws in the wind. Sometimes they even had spies."

He turned to Llewellyn.

"Pete, you'll soon be seeing some of that kind of thing, I expect. Or I assume. You will be working with other clergy on this thing? Right? And with the Grace Church people? Rebuilding and such?"

"Yes. Several of us have already been in touch."

Colville sipped again.

"And then there were the people who were caught in the middle," he said. "This was especially difficult in the smaller communities. People had lived there for generations, and they weren't equipped to live anywhere else. They knew they weren't likely to be victims, because they weren't black or Jewish or whatever the target group was. But they were troubled. They knew what was happening was wrong. They couldn't fight it openly. They didn't dare. They had families. Children who had to keep on living there. But they would talk, discreetly, to people like me. They didn't have to say much, or even know much. They knew the rhythms of everyday life. They knew if there were little tics in it. This guy's truck was gone all day. That guy had a group over when he should have been working. I'd get a piece of the puzzle from this one, and another piece from that one, and eventually I had a picture."

He gazed across at Llewellyn, sideways at Lew Perry.

"And they were afraid. Oh, my God, were they afraid. Of being pressed to join in the violence of the thugs. Of being noticed for not joining in. Of having a friend hurt. Of having a loved one or a friend cross over to the bad side of the line. Of losing what was best in their communities and having to live with it. Of having their children doomed to live with a hangover of hate. They were all terribly afraid."

He returned his gaze to the tabletop.

"So, yes. I had my sources."

Lew pointed to Colville's hand. The knuckles were white against the whiskey glass.

"You make it sound like it's personal. To you, I mean. Personal to you."

"It *is* personal. If you have any compassion, and you watch bad people make entire towns afraid, it becomes personal."

Lew finger-tipped a brief, staccato interlude on the tabletop.

"Ames," he said, most of that was before my time, granted. But this doesn't seem to have quite the same feel. It's not any kind of group violence, not some kind of wider thing. So far all we've got is one lunatic."

"That's true, as far as it goes. But I don't think the distinction matters much to the people who had pieces of their lives invested in Grace Baptist Church. And I don't think it will matter much to anyone if this guy keeps his promise to burn down a building with people in it. There's a kind of hatred loose here. It's racial, and it's poisonous."

He turned to Llewellyn.

"Pete, what are you going to be up to with the church people?"

"Well, rebuilding is the first thing. Fundraising and volunteer recruitment to replace the church. The clergy association is putting things together. And there will be support groups and other kinds of counseling for members of the congregation. Bob Greenlee says some of his parishioners are pretty badly traumatized. The older ones remember the old days. The younger ones have parents or grandparents who remember them. It's bad business, Ames."

"Very bad. Pete, as you move among these folks, you're going to hear things. Hunches, snippets of information. Anything could be important to finding the person -- or persons -- behind this. I hope you'll keep me posted. No item is too small to mention."

"You can count on it."

"Lew, I'm going to be gone for a while. You'll have to put the paper out without me. You'll always be able to reach me on my cell, but I may not be able to be of much use."

"I've got it. Don't worry. But right now, I do have one more question."

"Shoot."

"The Gandy Dancer's real name. What is it?"

Colville loosed a bitter chuckle.

"He goes by 'Dolph Rae.' His full first name is 'Adolph.' That's 'Adolph' ending in 'ph.' His father meant to name him after Hitler, but the malignant bastard didn't spell it right."

Chapter Four

Truth to tell, Billy Wakefield liked Jimmy's pretty much inside and out. The bricks, the ivy, the red doors curving up to a peak -- they reminded him of cool pictures he'd seen of England. Inside, at the right time of day, the sunlight through the stained-glass windows made it look like somebody had painted the floor all kinds of colors.

The Sunday service was like a pageant. And there was a part for everybody to play. Stuff for everybody to do. It wasn't like Sammy's church, where mostly you sat there and listened to the preacher talk.

Sammy's preacher seemed to enjoy his own talking about as much as anyone else was likely to. It occurred to Billy that this was not a very kind thing to think. He wondered if he might be *harboring a thought.* He'd heard grownups say that about thinking something they didn't want others to know they were thinking, but they were thinking it anyway. Billy sure didn't want anyone to know he was thinking unkind thoughts about Sammy's preacher, because he suspected maybe that wasn't quite as innocent as having to pee during the sermon. But he kept on thinking it.

For Billy, the hymns at Jimmy's were something Mom would call a *mixed bag.* Some of them were pretty dull, and hard as the dickens to sing. But some of them were way cool. He liked the ones where the choir rocked back and forth and clapped hands. He especially liked the one that went ...

One for the little bitty baby
Two for Paul and Silas
Three for the three men riding
Four for the four knocking on the door

When the choir got into rocking and clapping, pretty soon everybody else was doing it, too. Even old Mrs. Peabody would sway a little bit. But then she would jerk to a stop and glance around, like she was afraid somebody would see her doing it. Everybody knew -- because Mrs. Peabody made sure of it -- that she didn't approve of hymns that weren't from the regular old hymnal. Mrs. Peabody seemed to think it was some kind of rule that you shouldn't sing anything that wasn't from the regular old hymnal. Billy thought that Mrs. Peabody seemed to like rules a lot. He certainly hoped so, because she didn't seem to like anything else.

Once, in the car on the way home, Billy asked why Mrs. Peabody always seemed to be so grouchy. Dad said, "Because she's worried that somebody somewhere is having fun."

Mom said, "Bill," in that low, serious way of hers. But she put her hand over her mouth, and it looked like she might be smiling. Dad chuckled on and off all the way home.

There were two places at Jimmy's that Billy liked a lot. One was the library. Some of the books in there had pictures in them that looked like paintings. Billy especially liked the ones where people were kind of looking up into a light and smiling like they were looking at the most beautiful thing anybody could imagine. They made him wonder what it would be like to be in the picture with them.

Other books in the library didn't have any pictures at all. They were all gray and packed with words that were fancy-sounding and hard to read. Billy thought a lot of other people must find those books hard to read, too, because whenever he opened one of them, they were stiff and creaky, like maybe they hadn't been used a lot.

Billy liked to mess around in the library, sort of looking at whatever caught his eye. Father Pete called it *browsing.* He would take down a book for no particular reason and see what was inside. Sometimes they were dull and he'd put them right back. But sometimes they had really interesting stuff in them, and he would sit down and lose track of time.

One of his favorites was a great big Bible that was so heavy he could hardly lift it. There were no pictures, but there were flowery decorations down the edges of the pages. Billy liked to flop it open wherever it happened to fall and put his finger down on a page. Sometimes the language was so odd and old-fashioned that he couldn't make head or tail of it. But sometimes, if he said the words out loud, the sound of them reminded him of music.

The other place at Jimmy's that Billy liked a lot was Father Pete's office. He liked it because it was totally messy. One time Billy asked Father Pete if he'd been lucky and his Mom didn't make him clean up his room when he was a kid. Billy's Mom made a sound like she had swallowed something. Father Pete laughed so hard he had to sit down.

In Father Pete's office, stuff was stacked everywhere. There were papers and there were books. There was a place for Father Pete to sit behind his desk, and a couple of places for visitors to sit in front of it. In one space on a wall there was a picture of a dove flying up, and in another there was a cross made of driftwood, and that was about it. Everywhere else was full of shelves or stuff lying around. Billy felt like you could sit in the middle of Father Pete's office and close your eyes and reach out wherever you liked and be pretty sure of touching something interesting.

On the day of their visit, Billy was glad they met in Father Pete's office. After they'd said their hellos, Dad just nodded, like he was saying, *Go ahead, speak for yourself.*

"I understand you've got some questions for me," Peter Llewellyn said.

"Yes, sir." Billy said. "There's some things I just don't understand."

"Your Dad says you've been asking about the church burning."

"Yes, sir. It's been bothering me. I just don't understand how God could let something like that happen. My Mom and Dad said it would be OK if I asked you about it."

"You want to know why God lets bad things happen."

"Yes, sir."

Father Pete rocked back in his chair and laced his fingers together on his chest.

"Well, Billy, you've got a lot of company wondering with you about that one. We'll talk about it, but the short answer is, I don't know."

"You don't know?"

"No."

"But you're a priest."

"Priests are human, too, Billy. We don't have all the answers. Sometimes the best we can do is to help people see a way of thinking about things."

"Oh."

"So, let's talk about your question. You and your Dad are pretty tight, right?"

"Yes, sir. My Dad is great."

"You know that he loves you, right?"

"Yes, sir."

"Does he tell you how to do every little thing, or does he maybe even do lots of things for you? Does he come in your room in the morning and tell you how to comb your hair? Does he do your homework for you?"

"No, sir. My Dad says he wants me to learn to do things for myself."

"So, sometimes you make mistakes, right? And that can be pretty frustrating."

"Yes, sir. I'm not sure I'll ever learn how to tie a necktie. I mean, I don't really wear a necktie like grown men do, but someday I will, and I thought I should be ready, so I asked my Dad to buy me one and let me learn how to tie it. It's really confusing."

"So, your Dad gives you room to do things on your own. I mean, with more than neckties?"

"Yes, sir."

"Do you ever do things you know he wouldn't like?"

Out of the corner of his eye, Billy could see Dad wearing his *go-ahead* grin.

"Yes, sir. Sometimes."

"Why?"

"To try them out, I guess."

" Does he find out?"

"Sometimes."

"And how does that work?"

"Well, it makes him kind of sad."

"And what happens then?"

"Mostly we talk about it. Sometimes, if I've done something really dumb, I have to take a time out."

"And what do you do in the time outs?"

"Mostly I think about what I've done -- and probably wish I hadn't done it."

"None of that has to happen, you know."

"None of what, Father Pete?"

"Your Dad doesn't ever have to be sad, and you don't ever have to be sorry about something you've done."

"I don't understand."

"He could just tell you how to do everything. Even little things. He could write a lot of it down, so you'd kind of have a script to follow. And then everything you did would be jake with him. Everything and always. Because you would always be doing exactly what he told you to."

Billy had to take a minute and think about that one. Dad could always tell when that was going on, because Billy got a certain kind of expression on his face. Dad would give him a minute and then say, *I see you're chewing on something. Can I help?* So, yes, Billy did have to chew on that last thing.

Finally, he looked up.

"I don't think that would work very well, Father Pete."

"Why not?"

"Well, because then I sort of wouldn't really be me. Dad wouldn't ever be able to be proud of me or anything. When we did things together, we wouldn't really be doing them together. It would just be him doing things and me being sort of like a robot or something."

"So, does all this maybe give you a way of thinking about your question?"

"I'm not sure I understand."

"Well, as near as I can tell, God wants us to be ourselves. He wants us to live in a certain way because we decided to do it on our own, not because He forced us to. That means we have to be free to make mistakes and even to do bad things. Some people abuse the freedom and do very bad things. But God still doesn't take the freedom away."

"I'm going to have to think about that one, Father Pete. I'm going to have to think about that one a lot."

"I'm sure you do, Billy. And some days you'll think it isn't much of an answer at all. But if you work at it, if you think hard about it, some days you'll feel like it helps. Now, why don't you get some library time while your dad and I go down to the kitchen for a cup of coffee?"

Billy grabbed the cue and scampered away.

"Do you think I helped him?" Peter Llewellyn said in the kitchen.

"My guess is you did. I'll let you know." Bill Wakefield said.

"Boy likes books."

"Gets it from me, I guess. I was always a reader. Guys at work call me *professor*. You can't beat a good book."

"How's the investigation going? The church burning. I assume they keep you guys posted."

"Yes, they do. This guy's going to be a tough one. He had the place rigged just right to be beyond saving by the time we got there. The ignition device appears to be home-made, from parts you could get anywhere."

"I understand that one of your colleagues got hurt."

"Yes, but not badly. Toby Butler. Friend of ours. Billy calls him *Uncle Toby*. Ran into the church before anyone could stop him or help him. Beam fell on him and banged him up a little. He'll be all right. He said afterward that he thought he heard someone in the church. Toby's kind of the runt of the litter at work, and sometimes I think he tries too hard to prove himself."

"I guess Sarah Jane is probably uptight about all this. About your safety in arson fires."

"Yes. I try to ease her mind, but it doesn't help much. You said your friend Ames is poking into the thing? The newspaper editor?"

"Yes. A white supremacist the feds were watching has gone off the radar. They are worried. Ames is helping to look for him."

"Who is the guy?"

"The federal people nicknamed him The Gandy Dancer. To make a living he does itinerant track maintenance for the railroads. His real name is Adolph Rea. He styles himself as a kind of redneck philosopher. Apparently, he's a savant. Very articulate, very

well read. He cherry picks and slants the obvious writers.
Nietzsche, Machiavelli. Ames says he could probably write a pretty
good treatise on Social Darwinism. He's a real hate-monger. He's
never been caught personally doing anything illegal, but he seems
to be nearby a lot when something happens. Just before or just
after."

"And the federal authorities think your friend can help them
find this guy?"

"Not the authorities. Someone else. His name is August
Hood. He is a free-lance investigator of sorts. He works with his wife
and her father. And they would have a personal interest. They're
black."

"And they think your friend can do something that federal
investigators can't?"

"Ames was a top reporter in the civil rights era. He still has
contacts."

"I hope they're good ones. I have a very bad feeling about
this business."

Chapter Five

        I should write a manifesto, I suppose. I will want to have one someday. For the record. So I guess I should start making these notes. Jot down some ideas, so I can think about them, smooth them, polish them.

        The Lilliputians will want to know, *why?* They will want to know why I shook their world. And I guess the answer is, *Because I can.* That's sort of the point of the thing, after all. That's what the strong man is about. He does what he does what he does because he can. And because he is called upon to do it. I am called upon to be their Howard Roark. Destroying the tacky little order they thought they had established.

        Howard Roark. That's a nice touch. I will include it in my manifesto. They will have to look it up, of course. They shouldn't have to, if they read more than the sports pages and the labels on their beer cans. But they don't, and so they will.

        Starting with the church was a nice touch, too. Even God can't stop me. That's what it said. And sure enough, it provoked their so-called leaders to jump up and start moralizing about justice. Hah! Justice. Strength is what matters. I will show them that. When their so-called leaders can't find me and stop me. When their so-called leaders are shown up for what they are -- fools and weaklings. When I show that the tacky little order they love can't protect them. Not from the strong man.

        The Lilliputians also will want to know, *Why now?* Because my time has come, that's why now. I am Claudius seizing his moment after a lifetime of hiding in his own skin. Of course I am Pollios, too. My own Pollios. I realized early on that if others sensed the strength that would blossom in me, they would try to nip it in the bud. So, my inner Pollios told me to become the outer Claudius. Two in one. Two for the price of one, so to speak. And the price will be high. Ever so high.

        Claudius and Pollios. Another nice touch. I think I will include them in my manifesto, too. Of course, the Lilliputians will also have to look these up. Off to the reference books, folks. That's how we learn.

But in the final analysis, I am Omega. The end. For Omega, the end of sniveling and pretending. For the Lilliputians, the end of peaceful delusion. They will deal with me, now. They will learn about reality, now. They will learn about strength. And they will learn about death. The end must include death. Omega. The ultimate end. The true strong men always show that they are willing to be instruments of death.

But not right away. Not yet. Not now. I must draw the lessons out a while. Soon it will be time for another display, and another note. What shall I do this time? Another church? I think not. The best target among those was the one I've already done. A school? Maybe. But maybe not. I'll have to think about it.

And what shall I say in my message? A longer one this time, I think. Lift the skirt a little. Show a little leg. Tease. How shall I begin?

Well, Lilliputians, as you now know, I'm back. I can hear you asking yourselves Who is this fellow?

Actually, you think you know me. I am among you. One of you. But you don't really know me. I am your Claudius. You've thought you could ignore me. Overlook me. As you are now learning, you can't.

Not bad for starters. I'll have to develop it a little more. And YES!!! I'll give them a deadline. Talk about a tease. But what kind of deadline? It should be one with meaning. I'll have to think about that one, too. What would Claudius do?

And what will Omega do? Two copies of the message next time, I think. One to the fools at the television station, of course.

And one to the fire department. A nice touch.

Talk about a tease.

Chapter Six

Ames Colville parked down the road and eyed the house for a while -- a sturdy old clapboard farm house with a tin roof and a covered porch running across the front. It had a central hallway, he knew, reaching unbroken from the front door to the back door, positioned to let prevailing winds blow through it. Bedrooms and sitting rooms lined either side. At the back were a big kitchen and a dining room centered on a huge, round oak table. In the middle of the table was a lazy susan worn shiny at the edges by countless hands.

He pictured the generations of Carolina yeomen who'd lived there. The early ones, he knew, used an outhouse and raised their well water through a hand pump on the back stoop. They slept on feather mattresses. In the summer they pulled the heads of their beds into the hallway to be cooled by night breezes. On winter mornings they sprinted to the midpoint of the hallway, where they'd left clothes hanging near the oil-burning stove that was the house's main source of heat.

Over the years since, the house had been wired and plumbed and climate-controlled. His friends lived there now. Just the two of them. Four children had grown and moved to their own places. Arthur and Lacie Godwin stayed in the big old family home because it was the family home. The hand pump on the back stoop no longer worked, but they kept it there because it was part of the place. Though the kitchen had modern appliances, they also kept the big iron brute of a coal-burning cookstove. Lacie made some dishes the old way, and she needed the coal fire for those.

Arthur and Lacie were the first in their families to escape the merciless labor of small-farm tobacco-growing. Arthur ran a small country store and gas station. Lacie helped in the store and tended a quarter-acre vegetable garden. They grew much of their food, because that was what people around there had always done. They killed a pig in the fall and put the meat up themselves.

Ames started the car, eased between two patriarchal oaks that flanked the top of the driveway, and parked in a sandy dooryard. The front door of the house opened before he could knock. A trim, white-haired woman emerged and bussed his cheek.

"Ames. It's always good to see you."

"Lacie. I'm a little early. Arthur's still down at the store, I guess."

"Yes, but he'll be here directly. He's anxious to see you. Let's sit on the porch while we wait. It's still warm enough while the sun's out. I made some of those pecan brownies you like. Will you have some iced tea?"

"I'd love some tea. But Lacie, you should be ashamed. Those brownies are an evil temptation for a fat old man."

"Oh, hush Ames. A few won't hurt you. Tomorrow's soon enough to eat rabbit food, if you think you must."

He settled into a wooden rocker. She brought the brownies and tea, and settled beside him.

"How have you been?" she said.

"Good. I've been good. And you two? Kids OK?"

"Everybody's fine. Another grandchild on the way."

"That makes -- what? -- seven?"

"Eight."

"Christmas is getting expensive at your house."

"At our age, we don't have much else to do with our money."

"I hear you."

"On the phone, you said there'd been some trouble down your way."

"Yes. A church burning."

"A black church," she said. It was a conclusion, not a question.

"Yes."

"My land," she said, with a small shake of her head. "I thought all that was behind us."

"Afraid not. The guy that did it sent a note to a tv station. Said he was going to do some more. Said one day he meant to do a place with people inside."

"Oh, my stars. You think there's some kind of connection up this way?"

"Don't know. Maybe. The federal people are looking for a man. Dolph Rea. He's one of those they keep an eye on. But he disappeared a while back. Went completely off their radar. They're nervous about it. They want to find him as soon as they can."

"I've heard the name, maybe. They think he did the church burning?"

"Not necessarily. But they think he may be agitating it, or at least know something about it. He's traveled the area. Talks a lot of hate. Has a lot of connections."

"Oh, my," she said, trailing off into pensive silence.

Ames gestured at a cloud of birds in silhouette against the distant sky.

"My goodness what a flock," he said. "Geese?"

"Yes. On their way to winter at Mattamuskeet, I expect."

A battered pickup rattled down the driveway and fetched up in the dooryard. From it emerged a lean and weathered man who was up in years but not yet bowed by them.

"Who's going to die first?" Ames said. "Arthur or that old truck?"

"The truck, most likely," Lacie said. "But Arthur might roll over soon after. He loves that thing."

Arthur Godwin mounted the porch steps and met Ames with a two-handed shake.

"Ames, you never get older," he said.

"Arthur, you never run out of bull."

After personal preliminaries and an update, Arthur Godwin got down to cases. "So, the government wants to find this man Rea, and they've asked you to help."

"Not exactly. The government does want to find him, but that's not who asked me to help."

"Oh? Who, then?"

"A friend down in Yaupon Bay."

"A private citizen? "

"Yes, in a way."

"What do you mean, 'In a way'?"

"I guess you'd call him a private investigator of sorts."

"And why is he mixing into this particular thing?"

"He gets into a lot of different things. Whatever interests him. He's independently wealthy, so he can do pretty much what he likes. He calls himself a problem-solver. Usually he's trying to help people who've gotten into some kind of trouble. In this case there's an extra consideration. He's black."

"Oh," Arthur said, reaching for a second brownie. "And this man thinks you and he can accomplish things that federal agents can't?"

"Well, yes, actually. He works with his wife and her father. They're pretty effective. She's a computer expert. Her father is a retired ballet dancer. He retired early. Not a lot of market for black ballet dancers in his day. He stays in physical shape. He does their legwork. He's -- well, frankly, he's a second-story man."

"Oh, my," Lacie said.

"And if they find Rea?" Arthur said.

"Hood -- that's my friend's name -- thinks he can make Rea tell what he knows about this church-burning business."

"Your friend Hood must think he's pretty persuasive. Men like Rea aren't real talkative to investigators."

Colville struggled up out of the rocker and arched his back. He circled his chair to stretch his legs. He settled back down.

"You're going to think I'm nuts," he said.

"I doubt it."

"As a boy, Hood spent several years on a family plantation in the islands. The overseer there took him under his wing. Became a sort of surrogate father. Hood's had deserted his mother when she was pregnant. The overseer took Hood back into the interior. They spent some time there. Hood learned some of the ways that only the oldest of the old people knew. He can get into someone's mind. Make them see things, do things, tell things."

Arthur's eyebrows went up. "He puts spells on people?"

"Yes. Sort of."

"I've heard tell of that," Lacie said. "Some of it came up through the low country down below Charleston. Some people down there still paint their door and window frames blue to keep the boo-hags out. He has to have something from you, right? A hair, a piece of dandruff, a drop of sweat. But if he has that, he can spell you."

"That's about it."

Arthur Godwin murmured something wordless, rocked back in his chair, gazed at the treetops.

"So," Ames Colville said, "are any of the old troublemakers still around?"

"You think they might know Rea?" Arthur Godwin said without lowering his gaze.

"Maybe."

"Oh, they're still around all right," Godwin said, looking back down. "They don't do any real troublemaking any more. Times have passed them by, and they know it. County sheriff's a young black guy. Hell, some of them have grown grandchildren."

"So they're up to nothing?"

"They meet every once in a while. Beat their chests about white supremacy. Assure each other that the world is going straight to hell. But that's about it."

"You think they might still be in touch with others?"

"Possibly. Once I did hear a couple of them in the store talk about giving money. Making donations."

"Who would they be giving money to?"

"I don't know. I guess there's a few hate groups around that would accept your check to promote their cause."

"Could you get me a name?"

"I might be able to do that. Could take a couple of days, though."

"That's OK. I'd be obliged if you'd try."

"I'll do my best."

"Will you stay for supper, Ames?" Lacie Godwin said.

"Wish I could, but I have to be in Yaupon Bay. I'd like to get back there before dark."

As he started forward his chair, she put her hand on his forearm.

"Ames," she said, staccato. The polite equivalent of saying *stop.* "Earlier, when I asked you how you've been, you turned away from me when you answered. So let me ask you again. How are you?"

Colville settled back in his chair. "Waiting on a doctor thing. A lab report. Maybe cancer, maybe not."

"Oh, no."

"Could be nothing. But it's got me thinking."

"About …?"

"Retirement. I feel well. I think I'm probably healthy. Maybe I should put down the work and live a little while I still can."

"What would happen to the paper?"

"I've got a young man with me. He came down from New England to get a start with the company that owns the daily in Yaupon Bay. He got in trouble through no fault of his own. Hood helped him out. In return, Hood asked him to work with me for a year. Helping and learning. He's stayed two so far. He's got talent. He's got the instincts and the skills you can't teach."

"He would take over?"

"I would like that, but I don't know. He still has stars in his eyes about making it to the big city dailies."

"But you'd like for him to take over."

"Yes, that would be a good thing for the paper and for the town."

"And if he won't?"

"Well, if the lab report is bad, I guess I'd have to shut it down."

"And if you're OK?"

"I don't know. I'm still making up my mind about that."

"Take care of yourself, Ames," Lacie Godwin said. "See to your own welfare first. You can't do anything worthwhile for others if you don't take care of your own welfare."

"I'll try, Lacie. I'll sure try."

He turned to Arthur Godwin.

"You think you can get me that name?"

"I think so."

"You think you can do it without attracting any attention? I mean to yourself? These guys may be old, but I'd hate to have them drawing a bead on you."

"Yes, I think I can do that. Give me a couple of days. I'll get in touch, one way or the other."

"Thanks. Give me a rain check on that supper invitation. I need to catch up on Lacie's biscuits."

Chapter Seven

Ames Colville liked the space-ship image. Lew had said it first: Hood's house looked as if aliens had gone a mile deep into The Barren, as the locals called the vast coastal swamp that bordered Yaupon Bay, and beat back nature's tangled dominion to clear room for an edifice that was all planes and angles. The only made thing in a primordial world. Steel and polished wood forming stark lines and corners. Landscapes of glass.

Ames thought of spacecraft when he considered the house, and he thought of aristocracy when he saw Hood and Aimee together. Hood with his chiseled features and ramrod posture and eyes that could stop you and hold you. Aimee with a radiant grace that transcended mere physical beauty.

Ames settled his ample frame in an easy chair, sipped a Buffalo Trace -- double, with a single ice cube -- and watched them working shoulder to shoulder in their open kitchen. Aimee hummed a high, wandering melody. Hood worked in focused silence.

"What's tonight's menu?" Ames said.

Aimee looked up and beamed a smile.

"Citrus boiled tiger shrimp with Louis sauce; North Carolina trout with crab cakes and herb salad; sauteed asparagus and lemon zest orzo. The wines are La Crema pinot noir, La Crema chardonnay, and Bevan sauvignon blanc."

"Sounds delicious as usual," Ames said. "Will Larkin join us?"

"Yes. He's cleaning up. He spent the afternoon in the gym."

Larkin, Larkin ...

Larkin, who moved with such lithe economy that the full weight of his body seemed not to press down upon his feet.

Larkin, who disliked false courtesy: *My daughter accuses me of being rude, Mr. Colville. I hope I'm not. I simply do not enjoy the company of white people and see no need to pretend about it. To them I am a symbol or an object of pity or scorn. But never a man. I mean no discourtesy. You'll get used to me.*

Larkin, who was at his core a cultured and decent man who believed in fair play, hated wrongdoing and cherished his friends. Over the years of their acquaintance, Ames had come to like him and value his advice.

I've penetrated your disguise, Larkin. You're really a nice guy.

Don't tell anyone. You'll compromise my style.

Hood came from the kitchen, poured himself an Aberlour 16-year-old single malt Scotch, and took an easy chair next to Colville. Aimee joined them with a glass of sauvignon blanc.

"We have a few minutes," Hood said. "Can you tell us more about your health situation?"

"Well, the bare facts are that they took a biopsy and I probably have about a week to find out about the results. But, the situation? Well, the situation is that I walked into the doctor for the standard checkup, like I've done a hundred times. I had nothing on my mind but a few afternoon errands and maybe a little fishing on the weekend. Daily life. I went in ordinary and came out with the possibility that I'm a walking dead man. And you know what, Hood? It pisses me off. I know I should be afraid, and I suppose I am at least a little. And I know I'm not immortal. You live long enough, you're gonna get something bad. And dammit, I'm 70 years old. I'm not a fool, and I know this kind of thing comes with age. But it pisses me off, anyway. It just pisses me off."

"Careful Ames," Larkin said from behind him. "You'll blow a fuse."

"Come and have a drink with me, then. Consider it a rescue mission."

Larkin poured himself a Scotch, circled through the kitchen to bring the shrimp hors d'oeuvres, settled with the group.

Hood touched a nearby console, and a sound system began murmuring Mussorgsky's *Pictures At An Exhibition*.

"I assume," Colville said, "that by now you've assembled a dossier on Rea."

"Yes," Aimee said. She produced a file, opened it and passed a photo to him.

The young man was big and fit. Hair in a buzz cut, military style. Bright blue eyes looking straight into the camera.

You'd call him handsome, Ames thought, except that there was no grace in his face. There wasn't anything in his face except the physical features of it. No joy, no grief, no compassion, no cruelty, no mirth, no melancholy. The face said only that the human being behind it was precisely that -- behind it, out of sight and out of reach.

"I looked into the federal files on him," Aimee said.

"Without their knowledge, of course," Colville said.

Aimee beamed again.

"Of course. Here's his profile, at least as the government sees it. He's 28. His mother died young. He never really knew her. He was an only child. Grew up with just his father. The old man was a rough customer. A hater, a boozer, a brawler. He wasn't at home much, and he wasn't much of a father when he did hang around.

"Young Rea was never normally socialized. He grew up alone and angry. He took refuge in books. Read everything he could get his hands on. The old man died when he was 15. He took off and never looked back. He was big for his age, so he could lie and get the railroad work.

"He kept up the book habit. He is extremely well read and well spoken. He is probably quite bright. After a few years on the road, he began gravitating toward angry groups. Ultra-right-wing political people. White supremacists. He was outspoken and articulate. Attracted attention. He began to get invitations to speak at rallies. Became a celebrity of sorts. Began to style himself as a political thinker for the movement -- whatever the movement of the moment happened to be. Then became an outright agitator, at least in the eyes of the federal people.

"They could never catch him at anything illegal, or anything more than inflammatory talk, for that matter. But stuff tended to happen when he was around. Just bully-boy stuff in the beginning. Harassment and vandalism aimed at Blacks, Jews, and now of course Muslims. Auto caravans of hooligans through minority neighborhoods in the middle of the night. Things like that.

"But then, about a year ago, the government people began to notice a new kind of thing. Gun store burglaries. Fertilizer thefts. Not a lot of it, and nothing huge. Nothing necessarily more than ordinary police blotter fare, except for the timing. Rea was always nearby. They thought he might be escalating. And then about six months ago he disappeared. Vanished. No sign of him on railroad employment rolls. Not a trace of him anywhere.

"The federal people worried that he had gone underground for some specific reason. Another step of escalation. And then the church burned, and they got really worried. He was last seen at a white supremacist rally near here."

"Do they think he burned the church?" Ames said.

"Not necessarily. That would be a long leap even for him. But they think it's credible that he could have provoked it. And they think that at a minimum he'd have a pretty good idea who's doing it. They want to find him. Badly."

"And now," Hood said, "So do we. You said you had a name for us, Ames?"

"Yes. Daniel Doar. He's a lawyer up in Charlotte. Represents right-wing groups, tries now and then to peddle free-speech issues for the Klan, defends skinhead thugs who get into trouble. My friends up the road said this is the guy their over-the-hill hothead neighbors send money to."

"Any of your other contacts know about him?"

"Not yet. I'm still checking."

"Do your friends think this man is likely to know Rea?"

"They don't know about that one way or the other. But they say he's at least likely to know people who know people who know him. That sort of thing."

"It's a start," Hood said.

"How do we handle it?" Ames said.

"We'll begin by gathering data. Larkin can penetrate Doar's office and scan his files."

"That is," Larkin said, "I'll break in and steal information."

Aimee pulled a mock scowl. "Oh, Daddy."

" While he's there, he can tweak Doar's computer system so that Aimee can hack it from here. We want to know about the money he handles. Where it comes from, where it goes. Is he doing anything illegal, or is he just a banker for some unsavory people? We also want to try to get some idea of what kind of things he doesn't write down -- or at least doesn't keep in his office files. We'll have to visit him. Talk to him. Ames, I think you'll have to handle that. Obviously, none of us can try to chat him up about white supremacy."

Larkin coughed out a bitter chuckle.

"Well, yes. But also, I can't just waltz in and say, *Hi, I'm after the Gandy Dancer. I'd like your help, and by the way I already know a lot of your secrets.*"

"We will face that problem all along the line," Hood said. "We don't want Rea or any intermediaries to know that we are pursuing him. We will create a persona for you. You'll be a wealthy businessman who wants to support ultra-right-wing causes. I'll equip you with enough cash to get his attention. You want to meet people. You want to know where your money would go if you let Doar handle it. You want to vet Doar as a broker, and you want to vet the people who would ultimately get and spend your money."

"OK," Ames said. "I can do that."

"You'll wear a recording device," Hood said. "We will want to review your conversation with him very carefully. We will compare what he tells you to the content of his files. We will be especially interested in gaps. Omissions. They could help us prioritize our pursuit of the file data."

"How so?" Ames asked.

"You'll be a stranger to him. He won't trust you at first. But he'll want the money and the possible help in expanding his reach. So he won't turn you away, but he won't take you right to the heart of things either. Not the first time out. He'll try to test you and watch to see what happens. If we frame our questions carefully -- we'll help you with that -- and he omits in your interview information that we see in his files, that may point to material he doesn't want to show you right away. Insider information. Telltale information."

"OK," Ames said.

"One more thing," Hood said. "He will wonder how you got his name. He will ask you. I think our best tack there is to be mysterious. Give him the impression that you're not entirely the new kid on the block. That you have contacts and resources of your own."

"OK," Ames said. "But by the way, what about the money? Are you just going to have me give this scumbag a big wad of cash?"

"Oh, you needn't worry." Hood said. "Larkin can always steal it back if need be."

Chapter Eight

Peter Llewellyn watched the collection plate pass along the pews. From hand to hand. From story to story. From life to life. Touching like rain upon the just and unjust alike.

Front and center as always was Annie. Brave Annie, who faced with a smile the ravages of rheumatoid arthritis and the meddling of church biddies who thought that being Mrs. Peter Llewellyn made her community property. When his doubts roared and his spirits were at low ebb, he turned to Annie and was renewed by her cheerful courage.

Back one row and across to the far end, the plate passed to Mrs. Peabody. Lonely and frightened in widowhood, she clung to the liturgies of the church as if they were lifelines. In the congregation she was seen as a sour old prune. But in fact, she was simply afraid of happiness. She feared that -- like her beloved husband -- it would only be snatched from her.

Hand to hand, row to row, the plate reached the Wakefield family. Their bright, curious Billy would likely someday ask him the dreaded question: *Why did you become a priest?* It had come to him early and often in his ministry, perhaps because he didn't fit common stereotypes of priesthood. At first, he'd tried to answer, and found that earnest gazes quickly became glassy looks. If there was an effective way to explain being God-haunted, he hadn't found it.

Eventually he came to resent the question altogether, because it so often came from people who wanted an easy answer. A method to imitate. A mantra to let them avoid the hard work of bellying up to the meaning of the gospels. He often thought this sort would accept a talisman if he offered them one, and rub it faithfully for holy good luck.

Smack in the middle of the middle row, the plate reached Don Ruby, a pebble in the shoe of his ministry. Ruby was a smarmy hypocrite who cheated on his wife, neglected his children and reveled in ugly gossip. He was one of those who made Llewellyn wish that, along with hermeneutics and homiletics, seminary had taught him more about being a pastor to people you intensely disliked.

In his final year he had asked a mentor about such practicalities. About knowing how to navigate the swirling currents of parish life. The seasoned old fellow had limited himself to a single, sharp admonition: *You're about to become shepherd of a flock. Don't screw the sheep.*

Early in his career, Llewellyn had sometimes wondered why the church left important practicalities of ministry to on-the-job training. Later he moved toward the view that he sensed, in retrospect, his mentor had held: There was no formulaic classroom answer. Some lessons you could learn only by facing them.

Near the back now, the plate passed to Denny Albertson. He put nothing in. He posed as a feckless, disheveled, penny-pinching codger but in truth was an anonymously lavish donor to several parish ministries. He enjoyed throwing Llewellyn a mischievous wink.

Back row. Last seat. The plate reached Jim Polk. Llewellyn had once recommended him as a model to an interning seminarian.

Llewellyn: *You want to see a man of faith? You keep your eye on Jim Polk.*

Seminarian: *Why? Does he give a lot of money? A lot of time?*

Llewellyn: *No, not really. He gives what he can when he can. But he keeps his faith in the everyday of things.*

Seminarian: *I'm not sure I understand what you're telling me.*

Llewellyn: *The gospels are not about rules, or about some kind of scorekeeping in spiritual achievement. They are about the nature of love. They say we should love others as ourselves. But if you think of it in warm and fuzzy, lovey-dovey terms, we don't always love ourselves. Sometimes we don't even like ourselves very much. But we do always care about our welfare. About our safety and happiness and dignity as human beings. The gospels tell us we should care about others in the same way. People like Jim do that, from the way they treat their spouses to the way they treat the bagger at the grocery store and the geeky guy who's odd man out at work. They are careful to care. They are careful within themselves to guard against being envious or unkind. They understand that their relationship with God is reflected in their relationship with their fellow human beings. People like Jim work to do their best job of being themselves, in every ordinary minute of every ordinary day. They figure that if you are faithful in the little things, the big things will fall into place.*

As Jim Polk handed the collection plate over to the waiting usher, his face was shadowed by grief. Peter Llewellyn knew why. They had shared an afternoon working through the ashes of Grace Baptist Church. They had helped weeping parishioners retrieve the charred remains of Bibles and children's Sunday school craft projects. They had watched Pastor Greenlee -- himself weeping -- pour out consolation on soul after soul.

Peter Llewellyn and Jim Polk had worked, and they had grieved, and they had seethed. Llewellyn was seething still at such cruel misery being inflicted on innocent people by one twisted man. Not for the first time, he felt a red rage rising in him. And not for the first time, he wished that seminary had taught him more about another practical problem -- the problem of remaining, behind the vestments and the collar, subject to all the flaws of human nature. The problem, in Peter Llewellyn's case, of sometimes being swept away by aggressive rage.

Had seminary failed him on this score? Or was he such an ugly case that he couldn't be fully helped? For the most part he'd conquered the demons that made him seek an outlet in Navy boxing. But sometimes they came back. Sometimes, even yet, they were stronger than he.

And so, as the congregation rose for the doxology, Peter Llewellyn murmured a small prayer of penitence for what he knew he would later do. Late in their private afternoon at home, when Annie went down for her nap, he would call Ames Colville and ask to be included in the hunt for the Gandy Dancer. He would tell himself that he yearned to see justice done. But he would know in his heart that what he really wanted was a taste of revenge.

Chapter Nine

Daniel Doar was a pudgy, whey-faced gnome with eyes as cold as winter rain. He dyed his little remaining hair jet black and wore it in a lank fringe that sprouted just above his ears.

His appearance put people off. He knew that, and he liked it. He cultivated the effect with a sly-fox manner that he never dropped. His mantra for all comers was, *Keep 'em off balance.* No matter who you were, if you were going to deal with Daniel Doar, he wanted you back on your heels when you started.

He was therefore ill-prepared to deal with Ames Colville, who introduced himself as John Smith with a bland smile that said, *Yes, of course the name is phony.* John Smith was steady on his feet, thank you very much, and quite ready to deal with Daniel Doar.

"My secretary said you wouldn't tell her why you wanted to see me," Doar said.

"That's correct."

"Why?"

"Privacy."

"I charge for my time, even if it turns out I can't help you."

From a leather briefcase, Colville retrieved two wrapped stacks of $100 bills. He threw them into the center of Doar's mahogany desk.

"Let me know when we've used that up."

"That's a lot of money."

"I've got a lot of money. I've worked hard all my life. Never took a handout. I'm in a position now to give back. Help make thing better. This country's gone to hell, you know. People sponging off the government rather than work an honest day. People from God knows where pouring across the borders to get in on the gravy -- or to attack us in our own homes and communities.

" It's time for strong, hard-working men to stand up. To put things back in a proper order. To put the slackers and the takers back in their place. You know who I mean. Hell, nowadays you can't talk bad about somebody who's got so much as a suntan. But you know who I mean."

"Why did you come to see me?"

"I'm new at this. I need to meet people. Learn how things work -- certain things, anyway."

"How did you get my name?"

Ames gave him a long, bland look and a half smile. "I asked around."

Doar registered the rebuff and pressed on. "And what is your business, by the way?"

"Private. This has nothing to do with my business. Just with me. It's personal with me."

"Seems like maybe you want to ask a lot but not tell much."

"I want to make a difference, Mr. Doar. The kind of difference some people might not like. I don't want bad publicity for my company or for myself. There's nothing wrong with wanting some privacy."

Doar eyed him for a long moment. Nodded toward a crystal decanter and tumbler set on a side table.

"Drink?" he said.

"I don't mind."

"Bourbon?"

"Yes, please."

Doar rose to make drinks. Ames eyed his surroundings.

"Lots of pictures on your walls," he said." All those people friends of yours?"

"Friends, clients, people I met through my work."

"The fellow standing with you in that one there. Isn't he that Klan fellow from down around Louisiana? Gets in the national news every once in a while?"

"Yes. That's him."

"You know him?"

"We met at a rally."

"Seems like a good guy," Ames said. "Got some backbone."

"Cheers," Doar said, handing over a drink.

"Here's to making things right," Ames said.

Doar kept his eyes on Ames as he retook his seat.

"And so," he said, "just what kind of difference would you like to make, Mr., ah, *Smith*?"

"Well, for starters, I'd like to help get the right kind of people elected to office."

"Why don't you just go down to your local party headquarters?"

"I'd like to back some people who have the kind of views that you don't necessarily advertise or put in a party platform. For example, the kind of people who wouldn't get all weak-kneed if the police cracked a few heads from time to time. And the kind who don't believe that every scruffy bastard who can find the welfare office deserves a handout."

"And you think I'd know where some of those people are."

"Do you?"

"Maybe."

Ames took a long pull on his drink, set it on the front edge of Doar's desk, stretched back in his chair and laced his fingers together on his abdomen.

"And there are other ways to make a difference. I'd be interested in those, too."

"Meaning?"

"I'd like to meet some people who wouldn't shrink from taking a little direct action now and then."

"What kind of direct action?"

"Oh, a little night-time door-knocking maybe. Or maybe better yet, getting together some troops to make people think twice about clogging up public streets with demonstrations."

"Troops," Doar said.

"Just a word. A figure of speech. Men with guts and convictions."

Ames let another long pause pass by.

"And sometimes," he said, "it might be useful -- necessary -- to go farther."

"How so?"

"Some kinds of people need a real strong reminder that they should know their place. You read about that church burning down in Yaupon Bay?"

"Yes. Bad business."

"Nobody got hurt. Message got sent."

Doar put down his drink, leaned into his desk, propped his forearms on the desk blotter.

"Let's get right down to it, Mr. Smith. You some kind of cop?"

"Natural question. The answer is no. And I'm sure that if we reach the point of deciding to work together, I can convince you of that. Meantime, I have a natural question of my own."

"And it is ...?"

"You some kind of con man?"

Doar rocked back and scowled.

"Meaning what, exactly?"

Ames nodded toward the wrapped bills on the desk.

"I'm willing to spend the kind of money that would make that look like a lollipop fund. But all I know about you is word of mouth. One step above gossip."

"I figure I already passed one credibility test."

"What's that?"

"I didn't throw you out of here for the way you talked about the church burning."

"Yes, but you could take my money and bank it and tell me any kind of story about where it went, and what was being done with it, or would be done with it someday."

"So, what do you want?"

"I want to meet people, Mr. Doar. Your people. See them face to face. Feel the bumps on their heads. Get some sense of what kind of people you deal with down the line. What kind of people would be using my money. I'm good at judging men, Mr. Doar. I want to do a little of that here."

"And then?"

"If I get a good first impression, if I am satisfied, then I will do what is necessary to satisfy you, and we can go to work."

"Exactly where would we do this work, you and I together?"

"I'd like to begin down around Yaupon Bay. It could be a kind of base."

"You live there?"

"I have a vacation home there. I may retire there."

"And after Yaupon Bay?"

"I'd like to form a statewide network of people with common interests. Common commitment. I have the money."

Doar rocked forward again in his chair.

"Let's say, for the sake of argument, that I am what I say I am. That I know people who are ready and able to take a hard stand. That I could connect you with them. Can you explain to me why I should do that?

"You see, I don't know even as much about you as you know about me. I don't even have any gossip about you. All I have is a phony name, and your claims about yourself. So, why should I take the risk of doing what you ask?"

"All I want is to meet a few people. How much risk is there in that?"

Ames turned his gaze to the bundles of bills on the desk and let it linger there. When he looked up, he saw that Daniel Doar was gazing at them, too.

Without taking his eyes off the money, Doar took a pen and a sheet of paper from his desk drawer.

"All right," he said. "Give me 48 hours to set this up. Then call this number and ask for this man."

"Thank you, Mr. Doar. I'm sure you won't regret this."

Ames rose and scooped the money off the desk.

"I will take this with me -- for the time being."

Chapter Ten

The sound system delivered Elgar's "Enigma Variations." Hood and Larkin readied dinner in the open kitchen. Aimee set up a computer-driven projection system and lowered a viewing screen against a far wall. Ames lounged in an easy chair and sipped Buffalo Trace -- a double, with a single ice cube.

"What's the menu?" he called out.

"Lobster bisque," Hood said. "And lobster cobb salad. Parmesan crusted flounder. Wild mushroom spinach sauté. We have two wines you might want to consider. A Nobilo sauvignon blanc, and a Bollini pinot grigio. And it's ready for the table. Let's have dinner first. We can review the Doar situation afterward."

They moved to a round oak dinner table with an inlaid glass top. Hood and Larkin brought steaming plates, wine bottles and glasses.

"What was Doar like?" Aimee said. "Your personal impression."

"A toad," Ames said. "But a shrewd one. I couldn't tell from our conversation if he really believes in the stuff he represents, or if it's just an expedient way to make money. The cash you supplied me with certainly got his attention."

"Cash often does," Hood said.

Ames turned to Larkin.

"Did you find his office difficult to penetrate?"

"No," Larkin said. "Ordinary locks on the doors, standard safe. Nothing to suggest anything other than a working law office -- except for what was in some of the files. You'll see."

"The paper files were nothing," Aimee said. "Just garden variety civil legal work. The material that interests us was on the hard drive of his personal computer."

"You've reviewed the files," Ames said.

"Yes," Aimee said. "All three of us have examined them."

"And the headline is?"

"Several headlines, actually. Money coming in, money going out. Some of the sources and destinations are interesting, some are not."

"Huh," Ames said.

They finished dinner in silence punctuated by occasional small talk. Hood, Larkin and Ames cleared the table. Aimee readied the computer.

"Cognac?" Hood said. "Remy Martin XO?"

"I don't mind," Ames said.

They settled in easy chairs with their drinks. Aimee touched the computer, and the screen filled with ledger entries. She stepped to the screen with a pointer.

"We haven't had time for detailed analysis," she said, "but here's what is evident in a first pass. Doar's operation, if that's what we want to call it, is not huge. The kind of spending you hinted, Ames, would be quite an infusion for him. These are the records from his computer hard drive. The receipts are over here on the left. As you can see, they are small for the most part. But they add up. The receipts outnumber the disbursements, which are over here on the right.

Also, the dollar value of the receipts is larger than the dollar value of the disbursements. Doar is skimming -- or taking a professional fee, if you want to see it his way.

"Most of the disbursements are not particularly interesting. About what you'd expect. Right-wing committees of various sorts. Gun rights people. White supremacists. Defenders of the Confederate flag.

"But two kinds of disbursements do seem interesting. Look at these here. They are seasonal, in a regular pattern, and they are larger than many of the others. The giving corresponds to election years."

Ames craned forward and propped his elbows on his knees. "But I don't recognize the names of the recipients," he said. "They aren't any politicians I'm familiar with."

"No, they're not," Aimee said. "They are business people of various sorts. Some doctors and dentists. I'm willing to bet that when we check these names against campaign finance reports we'll find that Doar has been laundering right-wing political contributions through intermediaries."

"Makes sense," Ames said.

"Now, look at these other disbursements. They also are larger than others, and they are steady. Not seasonal. Every month."

"I don't recognize that name, either. Who is he?"

"He runs a self-storage facility in Fayetteville."

"Makes you wonder what he's storing," Ames said.

"Precisely."

Hood stepped to the screen and passed his hand from top to bottom. "These records are also interesting for what they don't contain."

"And that is?" Ames said.

"Dolph Rae's name is not here. And neither is the name of the contact Doar is sending you to."

"Clyde Hunter."

"Yes."

Ames sank back in his chair. "So," he said, "Rae is not part of Doar's network -- at least in the sense that he doesn't send or receive money. Or on the other hand, he's such a special part that Doar keeps the record of it somewhere else. Maybe even in his head."

"Yes," Hood said.

"And Hunter's name is not in these records for similar reasons?"

"Possibly. It' pretty much a given that he plays his own role somehow."

" So, who is this guy?"

"If the names check out as they appear, he's Doar's brother-in-law. A retired detective. Waylon County Sheriff's Department."

"How do we handle this?"

"He will want to test you. We want to make just the right impression on him. We want him to advise Doar that he should go ahead with you."

"And how do I accomplish that?"

"By testing him. The money gives you the upper hand. Doar is taking this second step with you because of the money. Make it plain that you are not willing to be the one who's getting tested. That the shoe is on the other foot. Spit in his eye -- figuratively speaking, of course. Let him perceive you as someone who takes it for granted that you are the tougher customer. Make him conclude that you are perfectly willing to take your money elsewhere if he doesn't persuade you that Doar's enterprise is worth your while."

"And how do I know when he's passed my test? The real one, I mean. Ours."

"He'll have to yield somehow. Maybe only a little, but he'll have to lift his veil without having succeeded in making you lift yours."

"And then?"

"You leave. On your own terms. Tell him you'll think it over. And I think you should also signal to him that while he may have passed your test, the next round is going to have to go a lot farther if you're going to play ball with Doar."

"Suppose he just isn't impressed?"

"We'll add a little sweetener. We'll make it possible for him to think he can check up on you when you've gone. We will equip you with false credentials you can use to rent a car. As an ex-detective, he'll know how to run the plates and check the rental. Aimee will slip the same identity into the corporate records files at the North Carolina secretary of state's office. We will show you as the principal of a financial holding company. We will make further details snoop-proof. With any luck, Hunter will see you as a high roller who knows how to keep his affairs private. That should be attractive to him, and to Doar."

"Meanwhile, for the face-to-face with him, I'm just John Smith."

"Right. You're John Smith, and if he doesn't like that you'll take your money and walk."

Ames went to a sideboard, poured another drink and lumbered back to his easy chair.

"Do you think it's possible we're barking up the wrong tree?" he said. "That Rae isn't in Doar's world at all?"

"Possible, but not likely, I think. And we won't bet all our effort on this Doar thing, anyway."

"What do you mean?"

"I want to identify whoever organized that last rally where Rae appeared. We need to find out what kind of contacts he had there -- and may still have."

"Shouldn't be hard."

"And there's more fodder here." Hood gestured at the screen. "I think we should pay a visit to that self-storage facility in Fayetteville. See what's inside. Then I think it's likely we'll want to pay the proprietor a visit. Have a little chat."

Larkin let out a dark chuckle.

"Meanwhile, we can cross check the identity of these intermediaries with campaign spending reports. Then we can have visits and talks with all concerned."

"They aren't going to want to talk to you," Ames said, "especially the politicians."

"Ah, but we have the magic phrase," Hood said, "the *Open Sesame.*"

"And it is?"

"We know where your money's coming from."

"Wouldn't that alert Doar?"

"I doubt it. He doesn't know we've penetrated his files. And he would certainly have no reason to suspect a connection between us and a man like John Smith. But you make a worthwhile point. We'll leave that part until we are farther along."

Ames' cell phone warbled. He fumbled it out of his pocket.

"It's Lew. Something must be up. He knows where I am, what we're doing."

Hood gave a mute nod.

"Hello. Oh, no. When?"

For a few moments Ames Listened in silence.

"It's longer? Huh. Maybe it's revealing. Can you fax it here? I'd like for all of us to read it together. OK. Thanks."

Ames closed the call and turned to the other three.

"There's been another fire."

"Where?" Hood said.

"The Martin Luther King Community Center."

"Damn."

"And there's another note. This one is a lot longer. Lew is going to fax it here, so we can go over it together."

They fetched fresh drinks while they waited. The fax machine whirred and put out two pages. Hood brought them to the dining table. When the others had gathered around, he read aloud.

"Well, Lilliputians, as you now know, I'm back. I can hear you asking yourselves, *Who is this fellow?*

"Actually, you think you know me. I am among you. One of you. But you don't really know me. I am your Claudius. You've thought you could ignore me. Overlook me. As you are now learning, you can't.

"But enough about me for now. We will get better acquainted as we go along. And I assure you, we definitely will go along. It's time to talk about people. Human beings. Human lives. I haven't taken any yet. But I will. I must do that, to finish making my point.

"*When,* you are saying. *Oh, when*? Well, I will be sporting about it. I will give you a little help. A deadline. November 8th. That's a good date. I will give you until then to find me if you think you can.

"But of course, you can't, because I am Claudius, and I am in the right. The world is meant for the strong, and I am one of them. The weaklings, the inferiors, must keep their place. Must be shown their place. I will make that point again with you from time to time, Lilliputians. Be nice to your firemen. But no death before November 8th.

"And then? On? After?

"You'll have to wait and find out.

"As ever,
"Omega."

The second page was a note from Lew Perry.

"The mayor is calling it obvious hate crime. He's asking for maximum federal help. The clergy association is talking about organizing citizen surveillance teams to keep an eye on logical kinds of targets. Some people in the black community are making angry statements tonight."

Ames tapped his finger on the Omega note.

"This is quite a garble," he said.

"And a lot of hostility," Hood said. "But of course, there would be."

"Lilliputians?"

"Tiny, nasty people with petty priorities."

"Claudius?"

"A Roman emperor," Hood said. "As a boy he had several afflictions. He stammered, he limped, he had nervous tics. Some in his family thought he was an idiot. According to one version of his story, a mentor advised him to emphasize his oddities -- even after they began to wane in adolescence -- to keep any of the ambitious people around him as seeing him as a rival for power. People thought he was a weakling. It was his camouflage until he finally did take power."

"And November 8th," Ames said. "Three weeks away. He seems to be making some kind of point of it. What's special about November 8th?"

"It was one of the days the ancient Romans opened the Mundus Pit," Hood said.

"The Mundus Pit?"

"Yes. They believed it led to the underworld. They opened it on certain occasions to make offerings to the underworld deities. And on those days the spirits of the dead came up to roam among the living."

"November 8th. The day they opened the door to hell."

"Yes. I fear we are dealing with massive hatred here. A poisoned mind."

"Three weeks," Ames said. "Three weeks to bring this guy down."

“Yes. But in his grandiose ramblings, he overlooks an essential.”

“What?”

“In the end, Gulliver couldn’t handle the Lilliputians, and Claudius’ enemies got him anyway.”

Chapter Eleven

Tip appeared promptly at tableside. "What'll it be, guys?"

Ames cocked a look at Peter Llewellyn and Lew Perry. "Another round of bartender's choice?"

The two nodded agreement.

"How's Annie?" Ames asked.

"As ever," Llewellyn said. "Brave. Cheerful. Mum about how much pain she's in. The doctors are pretty hopeful they can keep her mobile, but she struggles some days."

"Hug her for me."

Lew handed Ames a pink telephone message slip. "Speaking of doctors, yours called. Wants you to call back."

Ames pocketed the slip. "The blood test results from my checkup. My doctor's annual opportunity to whine that I drink too much. I'll call tomorrow."

Llewellyn shot him a hard look.

Ames kicked him under the table. "Let's get down to cases," he said.

"So the guy's name is Hunter?" Lew said. "The one you're going to meet?"

"Yes. Appears to be Doar's brother-in-law. Retired from the Waylon County Sheriff's Department."

"Where and when?"

"Lulu's. Tomorrow at 2. He wanted me to come up to Waylon County, but I insisted on Lulu's."

"Your turf, not his," Llewellyn said.

"Exactly. Making a point of it."

Tip re-appeared and set down their drinks. "Send up a flare when you're ready for another round."

Ames sipped, then tipped his glass toward Llewellyn.

"Pete, you said you want to help."

"Yes."

"I'd like you to come with me tomorrow."

"You want to take a priest to a meeting with a racist thug?"

"No. I want you to wear a muscle shirt and glower."

Llewellyn rocked back in his seat and struggled with a grin. "I see. Well, OK. Sure."

"He'll want to test me. I need to make a show of testing him. I expect it'll be a kind of Mexican standoff unless I can find a way to make him knuckle under. I have to do that. I have to make an impression that will convince him to tell Doar I mean serious business; that I'm not just some jumped-up wannabe."

"Well, ah, you want me to threaten him or something?"

"Probably not. I'm thinking you should go in early. Maybe half an hour. When I come in, wait until we're seated, then move to a place where you and I can see each other's eyes. If I need you, I'll signal."

"OK. I'll be there. Lulu's. Tomorrow, 1:30."

"Good. How are things with the clergy association and the Grace Church folks?"

"Busy. We've made arrangements for the congregation to meet Sunday mornings at the Big View movie multiplex in the North End Mall. They'll worship in one theater, hold their Sunday school classes in several of the others. We're rounding up donations of Bibles and Hymnals and teaching materials.

"The community college music department is letting them have a piano on
indefinite loan. Might even round up a little B-3 organ. I've made some space at our place for Bob Greenlee to have an office. It used to be a storage closet, but it's better than nothing. Oh, and the clergy association is organizing a foundation to receive donations to help them rebuild."

Ames gazed down at the tabletop. "Still organizing citizen surveillance teams?"

"Yes. That, too."

"Lots of ways that could go wrong."

"Yes. But we're not going to be able to persuade people just to sit on their hands."

"Ugly business. All this pain and sadness because of one twisted bastard."

"One that we know of. Others could be behind him. Obviously you and Hood think it could be the Gandy Dancer."

"Could be. Wherever he is, he's not up to anything good. You have any insights for me into the latest note?"

"No. The literary references are a jumble. No pattern that I can see. Just lots of hate."

"Could Rea have written it?"

"Not likely, if he's as well read and bright as they say."

Ames turned his gaze to Lew Perry. "The feds hit town yet?"

"Tomorrow."

"Sorry to leave you in the lurch at the paper. You doing OK?"

"Yes. I'm fine. You should know that I'm getting some pushback on that real estate story."

"How so?"

"Harry Carswell. He dropped in the office yesterday and treated me to his Foghorn Leghorn act.

Lew dropped into a fake basso profundo.

Son, I wouldn't dream of trying to tamper with the press. But as the president of your Chamber of Commerce, I have to be concerned with all the aspects of our community's welfare. And I have to tell you that I am distressed by some of what I'm hearing. I'm hearing that you may be trying to find out some private details of certain real estate transactions. And so, I have to ask you straight out. Is that true?"

"Harry can strut sitting down. What did you tell him?"

"I told him I was looking into some transactions but I wasn't at liberty to say more.

"And what did he say?"

"He tried condescending to the yankee boy."

Now son, I know you're not from around here, so maybe you don't altogether understand how things are in this part of the country. You see, we've been a poor region, and we've had to pull ourselves up. We have to work hard -- and, frankly, fight hard -- to attract business and industry to our communities. To attract jobs for our people, that is, and a growing tax base for our schools. Economic development is a very competitive thing between cities and towns down here.

Now, right now in Yaupon Bay we've got what you might call a public relations problem, with these arsons against the black community. Yankees -- pardon the term, son; I don't mean anything by it -- already think that every Southerner past puberty has a shotgun over the mantel, Klan robes in his closet and coon dogs sleeping in his bed, so we don't need any image problems on top of that. And we sure don't need anything else that might complicate a major economic development opportunity. I'm not saying anything in particular, mind you, and you can't quote me. But real estate transactions can be complicated and delicate, and it would be a shame for our community if you were to blow up a big one just because you wanted one more scoop.

Ames chuckled and shook his head. "So, clever Harry tried to cool you on the story by revealing that something big might be in the works."

"Yup."

"What did you say?"

"I told him I was grateful for his candor, and I would keep his advice in mind."

"What are you finding out?"

"More examples of what we already knew. A Charlotte law firm is fronting very quiet real estate purchases, one by one, all in the same general vicinity on the north side of town. They actually started over a year ago. I tried to talk to a couple of the sellers. They wouldn't say anything. Feels like they had to promise secrecy as part of their deal."

"Time to beard the lion?"

"I think it would be, if I knew who the lion is. I guess for now I'll have to settle for the guy who's doing his hunting for him."

"You're going to talk to the lawyer."

"Yes. I'm thinking that after I get this week's edition out, I'll drive up to Charlotte and see what I can get."

"Harry will probably have told them about you. Or one of the sellers, maybe."

"I'll just have to tough it out."

"Need help?"

"No. I'm good. You keep after the Gandy Dancer."

"OK. It's your story."

Peter Llewellyn leaned into their conversation. "If it is a big deal, and you expose it, you'll be taking a serious step."

"Yes."

"Do you worry about that?"

"A little. But I can't know how much to worry until I know what it is I'm worrying about."

"Have you thought any more about our earlier conversation?"

"About whether to stay here or go back to the dailies and aim for the metro papers?"

"Yes."

"I think about it all the time."

"Can I help?"

"Maybe. But I need to do a little more brooding on my own. It's a big life decision. I'm still working on how to make it."

"You're not the only one," Llewellyn said.

He ignored Ames Colville's warning frown.

Chapter Twelve

Ames had begun on the phone:

Hello.
This is John Smith. I want to speak to Clyde Hunter. Daniel Doar told me to call for him at this number.
That's me.
We need to meet.
Doar told me. Come on over here, and I guess I'll sit down with you.
No.
No, what?
I'm not coming to Waylon County. You're coming to meet me.
Why should I do that?
Because Doar wants my money, and he won't get it unless you do this my way.

A long pause. Heavy breathing.

OK. When and where?
Day after tomorrow. Two p.m. Lulu's near Yaupon Bay.
And exactly where is that?
Look it up.

Seen from above, the Yaupon Peninsula was a right-hand mitten hanging down. The back of the fingers and hand were covered by the great swamp. At the tip of the thumb was the town of Yaupon Bay. It was connected to the rest of the world by a single road that ran up the edge of the peninsula and onto the mainland. The locals ignored its official name and state route number. They simply called it The Highway. It was, after all, the only one.

Lulu's was an erstwhile road house with aspirations. It was the last watering hole on The Highway north of Yaupon Bay. Lulu had seen gentrification creeping her way and decided to try to catch the tide. Out went the Red Man chewing tobacco signs and the beer-stained pool tables. Out went Willie and the Merles Haggard and Travis. Lulu consulted her nephew -- a yuppie lawyer and the pride of his family -- on updating the music, the decor and the menu. He called it the *ambience.* She'd never bothered to look it up. He said it like it was important, so she figured it must be, and that was enough. She'd never heard the term *fern bar.*

The makeover was working by fits and starts. Old customers came out of habit and loyalty to Lulu. New customers came out of curiosity, or because they lived in one of the new housing developments springing up nearby. The result was a very unlikely mix of people who got along just fine in a live-and-let-live ethic. Lulu's nephew said the crowd was *eclectic.* She didn't bother to look that one up, either.

Ames spotted Peter Llewellyn in a black muscle shirt resting tattooed arms on the bar and nursing a tall drink. He spotted a lean, tanned man sitting alone with a beer in a back booth. Upper middle age. Erect bearing. Hair high and tight. He could have had ex-cop written on his forehead.

Ames walked straight over.

"Hunter?"

"Yes. Smith?"

"Yes."

Ames sat, and Hunter surveyed him with a neutral look.

"Beer?" Hunter said.

"I don't mind."

Hunter eye-signaled a server, pointed to his beer and to Ames. The server brought it promptly.

"So, Hunter said. It's John Smith, is it?"

"For now."

"What do you want?"

"I'm sure Doar told you about that."

"I want to hear it first-hand. From you."

"I want to help put this state back on the right track for hard-working white people. I want to see the coloreds and the whiners and the demonstrators put back in their place. I want the Jews and the Muslims to stay with their own kind."

"I mean, what do you want from me?"

"I'm given to understand that Doar brokers money for the kind of projects I'd be interested in. But all I have is second-hand talk. I'm prepared to invest a lot, if I can feel assured that it will be well used. Vigorously used. I told Doar I wanted to get a first-hand idea of the kind of people he has with him. I'm a good judge of men. He sent me to you."

"So I'm supposed to make you feel OK about doing business with Doar."

"If you can. I don't really know much about him. And I don't know anything about you."

Hunter pushed his glass aside, leaned forward on his forearms and flashed a feral grin.

"And we don't really know anything about you, do we, Mr. John Smith? You could be some kind of left-wing snoop. Or maybe you're just a fat old fuckup who thinks that having money is the same thing as having balls. You bring me into a lifted-pinkie saloon and slide into that seat like I'm supposed to take it for granted that you're some kind of big deal and just spill whatever you say you want to know. Well, that isn't the way it's gonna work, Mr. John Smith."

A hard-bodied young man slid onto the seat next to Ames and hip-checked him into the corner of the booth. His head was shaved bald, and he had a dagger tattooed on his neck.

"Who the hell are you?" Ames said.

"He's a friend of mine," Hunter said. "He helps me get answers to my questions."

Peter Llewellyn slid onto the seat beside Hunter, pulled Hunter's near arm onto the tabletop and slipped his own barred arm under the elbow.

"What?" Hunter said.

"He's a friend of mine," Ames said, "and he doesn't like this friend of yours."

"Now, you have two options," Llewellyn said in Hunter's ear. "Option one is that skinhead and I go outside and have a little together time while you and my friend Mr. Smith finish your conversation. Skinhead gets up grinning, and we stroll out like long-lost friends. Option two is, I break your elbow."

"Fuck you," the bald man said, and then paled as Llewellyn slammed a boot heel down on his instep.

"Option two would cause quite a ruckus in here," Hunter said.

"Depending on how loud you yelled. And anyhow, Lulu is my sister, and you'd be the one with the broken elbow."

Hunter flicked a nod at the bald man. "Go out with him. Wait there."

"Now here's the deal," Ames said when the two had gone. "Doar wants my money. Otherwise, he wouldn't have sent you to meet me. I don't need you. I have other options. But if Doar wants my money, you need me. Take it or leave it. One of us has to be the first to open the kimono, and I'm not going to do it. I don't have to do it. So, you can make me feel better about going ahead, or you can go back and tell Doar you blew the cash."

Hunter leaned back, folded his arms, worked his jaw muscles.

"Make up your mind, Hunter. I don't have all day, and I don't like this yuppie excuse for beer."

"There's going to be a race war," Hunter said. "No way around it. The coloreds and their kind will push and push until we have no choice but to defend ourselves."

"So what do you Doar people do? With the money he collects?"

"We prepare."

"Meaning?"

"We train people. We equip ourselves."

"How so?"

Hunter pulled from an inside pocket a folded photo. He opened it and passed it across to Ames. In it were a storeroom of guns, and Hunter standing in uniform before a Nazi flag.

"I'll take that right back," Hunter said. "I'm sure you understand."

"So," Ames said, "you have a room full of guns, a uniform and an antique flag."

"And more rooms like it. They're a start."

"And meanwhile?"

"We wait."

"For what?"

"Word. A signal."

"From who?"

"We don't know. Doar says we'll know it when we hear it."

"I'm not big on waiting. You could be taking steps. You could be preparing the ground."

"Meaning what?"

"That guy who burned the church and community center in Yaupon Bay. He's preparing the ground while you sit on your thumbs. Or is he one of yours?"

Hunter said nothing.

"Is he one of yours?"

Hunter said nothing.

"Belly up, Hunter. Doar gave you permission to open up with me, if you absolutely had to. Otherwise, he wouldn't have agreed for you bring that photo. And you wouldn't have brought it without his permission."

"Maybe he's one of ours, maybe not. I don't personally know. Doar is the only one who knows about everyone and everything. He keeps information divided up. Until now we haven't gone so far as that church-burning kind of business, but I suppose some of the other ones of us might have gotten a go-ahead to step things up."

"A go-ahead from who?"

"Doar, I guess. Or maybe there's somebody above him. It's possible."

"Doar's money. Does all of it go to you weekend Nazis?"

Hunter bristled and growled.

"Cool off Hunter. I'm in the driver's seat here, and we both know it. You can strut in front of a mirror when you get home, if it'll make you feel better. Does all the Doar money go for guns? Would that be the way he'd use my money?"

"No. Some of it goes for other stuff," Hunter murmured.

"Like what?"

"Fertilizer and stuff. You know."

"To make bombs."

"Yes."

"That all"?

"No. Some of the money goes to politicians."

"Which ones.?"

"I don't know. I don't think anybody but Doar knows. I've just heard him mention it."

Ames leaned back and surveyed Hunter for long, silent moments.

"So let me guess," he said. "Now you're going to tell me that you don't have more to tell me, because Doar keeps information divided up, and there's a lot you don't know."

"Something like that."

"So, I'll tell you a few things. You're going to go back and tell Doar I said our conversation was OK, as far as it went, but it didn't go very damn far. You're going to tell him I'm not a fat old fuckup, and that he has 48 hours to call me and take our conversation somewhere that matters. I want to get started on some work. I don't want to spend a lot of time going step by step with gofers who don't really know much. I want to meet some people who can look me in the eye and tell me in their own right that my money will be put to good and specific use."

"And if I don't?"

"My money and I go elsewhere. It's your job to convince him, and then it's his job to convince me. He has 48 hours. That's all."

"We done now?"

"Yes," Ames said.

He rose and left without another word. The skinhead shot him a glare as he crossed the parking lot and slipped behind the wheel of his rented Town Car.

"Let's sit here for a minute," he said. "Give them time to take down the license number."

"I think the goon already did that," Llewellyn said, "but yes, it won't hurt to be sure. Did you get anything good?"

"A little. They claim to be stockpiling guns and explosives. Preparing for a race war, he says."

"How's that supposed to start?"

"They'll get some kind of signal."

"From who?"

"He says he doesn't know. Somebody higher up."

"Somebody like the Gandy Dancer?"

"Could be."

"How did you leave it?"

"Doar has 48 hours to call me and take me through a next step. And it's got to be a good one."

"Think he will?"

"Could be. I figure your performance might persuade them I'm not a patsy, and the phony identity Hood cooked up for me could persuade them I'm not a left-wing snoop. You were pretty good in there, by the way. Learn that in seminary?"

"No. Navy shore leave."

Ames fished a cellphone out of his pocket and held it to his ear.

"Want me to step out?" Llewellyn said.

"No. I just want it to look like I'm doing something while we sit here."

"While you've got that in your hand, you could return your doctor's call. Unless you've already done that."

Ames sat silent.

"Have you done it yet?"

"No."

"Why not?"

"I'm not ready to deal with the answer."

"But it could be good news."

"I'm not ready to deal with the implications of the answer, no matter what it is."

"I don't follow."

"I've been careless about my end-of-life years, Pete. Thoughtless. I'm ashamed of myself. I've got some work to do with myself before I can make mature decisions about whatever the doctor may tell me."

"And you're scared."

"That, too."

"Ames, if the diagnosis is bad, you may not have time for fear. Why don't you come over to the church tomorrow and we'll talk about it?"

"Come on, Pete. I've told you how I stand on that kind of thing."

Llewellyn turned toward the side window and muttered under his breath.

"What?" Ames said.

Llewellyn turned back.

"Don't be one of the lazy ones, Ames. Belly up."

"You're angry."

"Goddamn right I'm angry."

"At me?"

"Ain't nobody else in the car, Dude."

"What do you mean, one of the lazy ones?"

"You want the scheme of the universe to be tidy, and when it isn't, you just declare that there isn't any scheme. You ignore your blatant self-contradiction and call that thinking. Bingo! Quick and easy answer. You save yourself the struggle of genuine thinking by decreeing there's nothing to think about. Goddammit, Ames. You're a better man than that. And too smart a man to hide in an intellectual version of free lunch."

"Churches are all fucked up, Pete."

"Of course they're all fucked up. They're full of human beings."

"They're supposed to be better than that."

"Says who? You?"

"Facts are facts, Pete. You can't deny it. You don't deny it."

"Yes, facts are facts. And here's one for you to chew on, my self-righteous friend. That business about that fellow Jesus going around saying he was the son of God, and dying and then coming back to life? All that actually happened. It's a fact. It's a verifiable fact, if you bother with the work of it. And the question is not what the Catholics or the Greeks or the Baptists or the Copts or the snake handlers and faith healers have made of it. The question is, what do *you* make of it, Ames. And I suggest to you that your decision is either to belly up to it, or be honest enough to admit that you're ducking."

Llewellyn opened the passenger door, stepped out and leaned back in.

"I'm out of here. Sometimes you really do piss me off," he said

He stalked away to his battered Subaru. Ames sat alone for quite a while before he cranked the Town Car and headed home.

Chapter Thirteen

Slick Hubbard had three rules in life:
-- Make a buck whenever you can.
-- Don't work any harder than you have to.
-- Stay out of other people's fights.

Fate had simplified rules one and two for him. Fate and the federal government, which decided to build Interstate 95 not a mile from the 80 acres of farmland that had been in his family for generations. With that, the Hubbard homestead was right beside the big highway that ran from where most of the country lived to where most of the country wanted to go.

Slick Hubbard had resolved to be unlike his father and the fathers before him. Slick did not plow and plant and agonize over weather and crop prices. He didn't ache from backbreaking labor that never ended. Slick, instead, became a businessman. He rented the place out. Hubbard's Acres became the venue for fiddler's conventions and rock concerts, motorcycle gatherings and RV festivals, revivals and gun shows. If you needed a place where a bunch of people could spread out and do their thing, Slick had your site. You might also smoke a little weed or even sell a little dope, if you were discreet, because Slick was a live-and-let-live kind of a guy.

Rule number three was pretty simple for him, too, because he didn't give a rat's ass about much beyond rules number one and two. So, when the guy with cash came along and said he wanted to rent a field for a white power rally, Slick was jake with it. He didn't have anything against the black folks, no. And he sure as hell didn't care about a bunch of loudmouthed shit-kickers. He just didn't give a damn either way, and cash was cash.

The shit-kickers came, and milled around, and drank from beer cans and bottles in brown paper bags, and ranted. They did get quiet when the one guy spoke. A little on the young side, Slick thought, and you might have called him good-looking except that there was something kind of missing in his eyes. He went on about how the future rightly belonged to white people and they had to

make sure it wasn't taken away from them -- which Slick thought
was kind of nonsense, since white people had things pretty much
sewed up already, near as he could tell.

But the young guy did have a way with words. Sounded like
he could talk the birds down from the trees, if he wanted to. So the
shit-kickers listened, and drank, and then finally went home. The
next day, Slick cleaned up the cans and the bottles and brown
paper bags and a few used condoms, and went on with business.
He didn't think again about the white power jerks until the black guy
showed up in the big Mercedes sedan.

The guy had a kind of glide in his walk, Slick noticed, as if
his feet didn't feel the full weight of his body. But the car and the cut
of the suit really caught his eye. They said *money.* And though the
pasture-renting business didn't include many style standards for
dress or conveyance, Slick was very fond of money and so had
developed a discerning eye for what money could buy. As the guy
approached the porch, Slick put down a Nehi grape and focused his
thinking on rule number one.

The guy's embossed business card (money again) said
simply *Fortis Fulmen, Consultant.*

"I'm hoping to speak with Mr. Hubbard," he said.

"That's me," Slick said. "How can I help you?"

The guy came up on the porch without being invited. "I'd like
to get some information about the white power rally you held here
back in April."

With that, Slick's focus jumped straight from rule number one
to rule number three. A black guy asking about a white power rally
wasn't up to anything Mrs. Hubbard's boy wanted to be mixed up in.

"I don't know how helpful I could be," Slick said. "They rented
my field, they came, they did their thing and they went."

The guy put down a gleaming leather briefcase and settled
into a heavy wooden rocker without being invited.

"You would know who rented the field."

"Don't remember. I'd have to look it up. A lot of people rent
my place."

"Would you do that, please?"

"Do what?"

"Look it up."

"Now look here. I don't think it's right" -- he glanced at the business card -- "Mr. Fulmen, whoever you are, for you to come right in here and demand to know details about my private business and the private business of my customers."

"I'll have to disagree with you on that. Did you attend the rally?"

"No."

"Just hit the sack and left them to do whatever they pleased?"

"No. I watched. From out behind them."

"One man in particular was among the speakers, I believe. A young man who spoke especially well."

"Maybe, yes, OK."

"What was his name?"

Slick squirmed in his chair, folded the business card in half.

"I don't know."

"You were watching, listening. You had to hear him introduced."

Slick studied the floor, said nothing.

"What was his name, Mr. Hubbard?"

To his own momentary surprise. Slick experienced a flash inside himself that felt something like courage.

"Now look here. I'm not having any of this. I'm not answering your questions. Who the hell are you, anyway, and why do you want to bother me?"

The guy leaned forward in his chair and put on a cold smile that made the flash inside Slick Hubbard wink right out.

"I'm someone with friends who don't like having their churches burned and their peace threatened. And I want to bother you because you are a reckless cracker bastard who helps a bunch of human weasels bother innocent people."

The guy dipped into the briefcase and brought out a nine-millimeter pistol.

"Now just a minute, "Slick said.

The guy placed the pistol on the porch rail and dipped back into the briefcase.

"Oh, don't worry Mr. Hubbard. I don't need the gun here. I have these."

He handed over a sheaf of photocopies.

"What the hell? These are my tax returns and business records. How did how get this stuff?"

"I broke into your office and photographed it."

"You did what?"

"I burglarized your office. Naughty of me, yes. But you've been naughty too, Mr. Hubbard, very naughty -- with the tax man."

"I don't know what you mean."

"Yes you do. Your business calendar shows an April event. But in the records you keep for tax purposes, there is no corresponding information. No record of payment. No evidence that the rally ever occurred. Was it a cash deal, then? Just a little green changing hands?"

"You're wrong."

"No I'm not. And I see a few other gaps as well. You've made a regular habit of accepting cash deals that you don't report for taxes. How much does it come to, Mr. Hubbard? Would an audit make you a candidate for serious tax evasion, or are you just a petty chiseler?"

Slick looked down at his hands and swallowed.

The guy leaned farther in. "Ah, I see. If the tax people got wind of this, you could be in big trouble."

"I don't know anything about any church burning, and I didn't help anybody do anything. I just rent land to people. That's all."

"Who was the man who spoke? What was his name?"

"You already know, if you know he was here."

"Stop sniveling and answer the question. Who was the man who spoke?"

Slick swallowed again, and heaved out a long breath.

"Ray. Something like that. That's what they said when they introduced him."

"Ray what? First name or last name?"

"Last name. First name sounded like *Dolf*. Crazy sounding name."

"Dolph Rea?"

"Yes. I think so."

"See, it's really good what you can remember when you try. Who invited him here?"

"I don't know."

"The man who staged the rally? The man who paid you the tax-free cash?"

"I really don't know."

"Like you didn't know Dolph Rea's name?"

"I swear, I don't know. Far as I know, he just showed up."

"Who was the man who set the rally up? The one who paid you."

"I'd never seen him before."

"And you just took his word for what he and his friends were up to? This total stranger. You were going to let them come onto your property and do whatever they pleased and trust that they weren't going to do anything that would bring down major heat on you? A white power rally is one thing. Free speech and all that. But how about handing off a major dope shipment? Or stolen cars? Or buying bomb-making materials? You're a lowlife, Hubbard, but you're not completely stupid. How did you protect yourself.?"

"I told the money guy I was going to watch them."

"What? And control them with mind rays? Spit it out, Hubbard. What did you do?"

Slick looked down at the floor, then back up. "I told the money guy he'd have to give me his car keys and driver's license until all the rest of them were gone."

"And you photocopied the license, in case heat came down later."

"Yes."

"This is later, and this is heat. Where is it?"

"I keep it in a personal file in my bedroom closet."

"Along with the copies of all the other licenses you held for cash-only deals."

"Yes."

"Because you didn't want them anywhere near your business files."

"Yes."

The guy reached for the nine-millimeter. "Let's go get it. I'll take this along. It makes me more comfortable."

In the bedroom, the guy eyed the driver's license.

"I want to meet him," he said.

"OK by me," Slick Hubbard said. "Just don't tell him I sent you his way."

"I won't have to tell him anything. You're going to get him to come here. I want to meet him here."

"What? Just go to see him. You've got his address there."

"Do you think a white supremacist is going to open his door for a chat with a black man? One or two questions, and he'll throw me out. You're going to help me. You're going to figure out a reason for him to come here."

"I don't want any part of this."

"I have your tax files. You'll do it."

"What makes you think he'll talk to you here?"

The guy flashed another smile. "We'll hold his driver's license and car keys until he does."

Chapter Fourteen

Before nodding off, Billy Wakefield reflected that Dad was right. The joint had been jumping at Jimmy's that day.

Dad and Uncle Toby and a bunch of other grownups sorted Bibles and hymnals for delivery to the movie theater. While they worked, Dad and Uncle Toby joshed each other, as they often did when they were together.

Toby, the next time you have a bright idea, remind me to discourage it.

You're just jealous, old man, because the chief jumped at it right away. Admit it. It really was a stroke to offer the fire stations as donation points for stuff the church needs.

That's what my brain tells me. My aching back wishes you'd kept quiet.

Billy liked to hear Dad and Uncle Toby joshing each other. There was a kindness in it. Billy had an idea that Uncle Toby could use a little extra kindness from time to time, because maybe people weren't always as nice to him as they should be. Mom and Dad talked sometimes about how he kind of felt like he needed to prove himself to the other guys at work. And Aunt Inez would scold him over little things -- like playing with the electric trains, as if that were some kind of really bad thing to do. Billy thought the trains were way cool. He didn't understand why Aunt Inez wouldn't like them.

And he didn't understand why anybody would want to be unkind to anybody else. It was even in the Bible. He'd discovered it there one day when he let the big old Bible in the library flop open and he put his finger down on the book of Job. (He learned later it was pronounced *robe,* not *rob.* The Bible really did have some funny stuff in it.) The language in the Job story was pretty old fashioned and not real easy to understand, but Billy thought he caught the basic idea of it.

God let a lot of really bad things happen to Job and his family. Job didn't understand it, because he'd always tried really hard to be a good man. Three of Job's buddies came to visit, and they told him it had to be pretty much his own fault, which was a long way from being the kindest thing they could have thought of to say. Job suffered a lot, and complained that he just didn't understand it and wished that he'd never been born.

And finally, God called down to him and pretty much said that he was God and Job was not, and that was about all there was to it. And although He let Job have a great new family and a lot of neat stuff, the story sounded to Billy like God was being unkind to Job just because he could. And Billy figured he just didn't understand, because God was not supposed to be that way.

He had never mentioned his confusion to any of the grownups. He kept it to himself, because he was afraid that picturing God that way was another example of *harboring a thought,* and he suspected it was not a good idea to do too much of that.

There was a lot of unkindness going around in Yaupon Bay, too, with the whole church-burning thing. Billy had tried and tried, but he just couldn't understand why anybody would want to be unkind to anybody else just because they were a different race. And he sure couldn't understand why anybody would go so far as to burn down someone else's church -- not to mention the community center. Billy didn't like unkindness, and there was so much of it in the air that it kind of darkened his days a little.

The church-burning thing was why the feds were at Jimmy's that day. That's what Dad called them. The feds. Billy wasn't sure what that meant, except that they were from somewhere high up in the government, and the mayor had asked them to come to town to help find the person behind the fires.

The feds were meeting in Father Pete's office with him and Pastor Greenlee. And although they were supposed to be helpers, they didn't sound very friendly. They almost sounded a little unkind. Billy couldn't help overhearing some of it, because of the way they were talking. Pastor Greenlee spoke for the local people, and you couldn't miss his voice. It was deep and rich and kind of round. Billy thought that if God had a voice, he must sound a lot like Pastor Greenlee.

One of the feds did all the talking on the other side. He wasn't exactly raising his voice, but he had put on that *now-you-listen-to-me* tone that grownups could get when they were fussing at each other.

Now, what's this we hear about your clergy association organizing some kind of citizen surveillance teams?

Well, that's about it. We're organizing citizen surveillance teams to keep an eye out for the start of more fires.

I don't like the sound of that.

Why not?

It complicates our work to have bunches of vigilantes running around. And it's just asking for trouble. One mistake, one angry moment of misjudgment, and somebody will get hurt, and you'll be responsible.

These people are not vigilantes. They are citizens keeping an eye on their own community's property. They have been very carefully recruited and coached.

I don't like it. It's not necessary.

And we don't like hearing that you people have been looking for the Gandy Dancer for six months, and you have no idea where he is, or if he's lighting these fires, or inciting the person who is, but here you are to keep on keeping on and we should all go home and not worry our pretty little heads. Of course it's necessary. You can't ask people just to sit around and do nothing when this kind of thing is going on.

Where did you hear about that? The Gandy Dancer. That is privileged information.

It's not privileged any more.

This is our investigation.

And this is our community.

I don't want to find out that you people have been hiding behind your clerical collars to take the law into your own hands.

And I don't want to find out that you people messed up the Gandy Dancer investigation, and then covered up the mess, and all this could have been prevented if you'd spent more energy investigating and less of it covering your bureaucratic butts. Exhibit

Billy caught sight of the feds when they left. They didn't look happy. He tagged along with Pastor Greenlee back to the little temporary office Father Pete had provided for him. Billy had some questions, and Dad said that there was no such thing as a stupid question.   Of course, he also said you always had to be polite, and Billy was very careful always to be polite.

He told Pastor Greenlee that he was still very confused about why anyone would want to set fire to a church or a community center. Mom and Dad had talked with him a lot about it, and they had been very patient, but it still seemed to him that it was just very unkind and didn't really make any sense.

Pastor Greenlee said that when people get filled up with hate they do things that don't necessarily make a lot of sense. And Billy said he didn't understand why anyone would dislike black people just because they were black, and Pastor Greenlee said, well, that's one of those hateful things that just doesn't make a lot of sense.

And Billy said he guessed a lot of bad things had happened to black people over the years, and Pastor Greenlee said yes, that was a fair thing to say. And Billy said, kind of like that man Job in the Bible. And Pastor Greenlee chuckled and said that was an interesting way to look at it.

And Billy said, *Don't you get angry? Like, when people burn down your church?   Don't you get angry at them?*

Pastor Greenlee said yes, he got angry. But he said it is important to forgive.

And Billy said (he was getting even more confused and figured he might as well say so) *How could you forgive that?*

Pastor Greenlee rocked back in his chair and smiled a great big smile and said that Billy had hit on one of the biggest questions there is. He said that if you return hate and anger for hate and anger, that all you get is more hate and anger.

He said that forgiving is not like forgetting, or just being silly and letting people run over you. He said that forgiving is like deciding you're not going to try to carry around a great big boulder. He said forgiving is deciding that you're not going to let yourself be controlled by a bad thing someone has done to you.

Billy noticed that when Pastor Greenlee talked about forgiving, he picked up a framed photograph on his desk and gripped it real tight and looked at it once or twice while he was talking. Billy saw in the picture a little black thing that looked kind of like a cell phone, only that was not quite what it was.

Pastor Greenlee saw him looking and said the thing in the picture was an electronic device that sent and received signals. He said it was the device that had been used to set off the fire in his church. A man had hidden it in the church, along with the materials for the fire, and used another device to turn it on from a long way away.

Billy asked him why he would keep a picture of such a thing. Pastor Greenlee looked at the picture when he answered. He said it was his reminder. He said that he imagined a man's hands putting the thing in his church and turning it on. He said it was his reminder that somewhere out there, a person -- a human being with hands and heart and feelings -- was so filled up with hate and anger that they had taken control of him. He said that the picture was his reminder -- Pastor Greenlee's own reminder -- not to be tempted to walk down the same path.

And so, just before he nodded off, Billy Wakefield considered that the day at Jimmy's had given him a lot to think about.

He was still saddened and confused by unkindness. But he sensed that a lot of grownups were, too, so he guessed he might be thinking about that for a long, long time.

He figured he might as well put the book of Job on a back burner for a while, as it seemed to present the problem of understanding God, and he figured that for the time being it was about all he could do to understand how to become a grownup.

Which reminded him of the joshing thing between Dad and Uncle Toby. He had seen other grownups do it, too. It seemed like a way for people to say personal things to each other without coming right out with it. If it was something grownups did, Billy figured he was going to have to learn it.

As he nodded off, Billy made a mental note to ask Dad to teach him how to josh.

Chapter Fifteen

With Larkin at his shoulder, Slick Hubbard was careful to stick close to the telephone script.

My name's Hubbard. I'd like to talk to Marvin Penny.
That's me.
You rented one of my fields back in April. Had a rally here.
Yes.
Took in some money, talked up some things you're interested in.
Yes.
Well, I've been thinking about that since. And if you don't mind me being straight out about it, I think I can help you make what you're doing a lot bigger deal.
How so?
Well, I rent land and pull crowds together on it. That's my business. And if you don't mind me being straight out about it, I'm pretty good at it. Now, that crowd you had here wasn't bad, but it could have been a lot bigger. You could get some big crowds here pretty regular, with my help. Take in a lot more money. And I see you were kind of the leader of that bunch you had here. Well, I say, better to be the leader of a big bunch than a small bunch. You could have some pull, if you worked at it and let me help you with it. Make a difference in some things.
How so?
Well, that would get us into some areas that maybe it's better not to talk about on the phone. My ideas, you know, which I kind of like to keep close to my chest. And I'm guessing from what I heard here back in April that you've got some ideas that maybe you wouldn't want certain kinds of people listening in on.
Maybe.
Why don't you come on back out here one day soon, and you and I will sit down with a snort and talk over how we can both make ourselves some money and do some good.
Well, I suppose so. When's good?

Before the meeting with Marvin Penny -- which seemed to him a limp-wristed kind of a name for a guy who was big as a house and about half ugly -- Slick tidied up a little. Ordinarily he didn't give a rat's ass about that kind of thing, but he did have to admit that the place had slipped a tad downhill since Adele took a powder with her *goodbye* in a sticky note on the fridge: *Slick, I'm not coming back. You can go to hell. Adele.*

He hustled out to the garbage with several empty vodka bottles and two issues of *Babes 'n Boobs Magazine.* He checked around the room for discarded underwear, as his and a lady's might land just about anywhere when things got up to speed. From the front hall closet he removed and hid some leather items that obviously were not made for farm use. Private was private, after all, and he knew that events of the afternoon would not likely proceed entirely under his control.

The guy who called himself Fulmen arrived early, still with that glide in his walk. He brought with him another guy, a big one who gave the name Marcus Lenta, looked like an African king, and silenced any questions with a look that went right through you.

"The meeting still on?" the Fulmen guy said.

"Yes."

"He's due here in half an hour?"

"Yes."

The big guy nailed Slick with that look.

"Sit down there," he said.

Slick settled onto the sofa, and spent the next 30 minutes thinking that sitting still and being quiet were damn good ideas.

The other two men rose when they saw a muddy F-150 rumbling up the long dirt driveway.

"That him?" the Fulmen guy said.

"That's what he was driving when he was here before."

"We will wait in the kitchen until he's all the way inside."

When Penny had come in and settled down, the Fulmen guy and the other one were quick. One minute they were not in the room, next minute they were.

The Fulmen guy crossed to the front door and locked it.

"What's going on here?" Penny said.

"We're going to ask questions, you're going to answer them," the big guy said.

"Who the hell are you?"

"Never mind. Do what you're told."

Penny shot a glare at Slick.

"You said we were going to talk some business. That's not this."

"He lied," the big guy said. "Sit still."

"No. I'm leaving."

The big guy nailed him with that look, and Penny fell silent.

The big guy did the talking.

"You are Marvin Penny."

"Fuck you."

The big guy leaned over close and looked him steady in the eyes.

"You are Marvin Penny."

"OK. Yes."

"You led a white supremacy rally here in April."

"Looks like you know I did."

"How did you organize it?"

"What do you mean?"

"I mean how did you organize it? How did you set it up, get people here?"

"I paid for use of the land, invited people here. They showed up."

"How did you invite them? How did they know about it?"

"I sent out notices."

"You have a mailing list?"

"No. Didn't mail them. Printed up some notices and put them around. Gave some to friends. They gave some to their friends. Posted some on light poles and such. Word gets around."

"So you don't have names. A list."

"Look here, whoever you are. I think I'm entitled to know why you're asking all this."

"You're entitled to know what I choose to tell you. Do you have a list with names on it?"

Penny tried to measure the Fulmen guy with a hard look, and it occurred to Slick that he might as well be trying to stare down a boulder. Something passed over Penny's face that suggested he had reached the same conclusion.

"Answer," the Fulmen guy said. "Do you have a list with names on it?"

"No."

"A man came and spoke. Dolph Rae."

"Yes. He was there."

"How did you invite him?"

"I didn't. He just showed up."

"And you just let him speak? At your rally?"

"I knew his name. I'd heard of him."

"You'd never met him."

"Not before, no."

"Do you know where he is?"

"No. He showed up, he spoke, he left."

"You collect money."

"Yes."

"How much do you charge."

"No set charge. I ask for contributions. Some give a little, some give more."

"How do you collect it? Personally? Are there checks?"

"I put buckets around. No checks."

"Checks leave a trail."

"You could say that."

"What do you do with the money?"

"It covers expenses."

"And …?"

"I give some away."

"To …?"

"People. Groups."

"Are you part of Daniel Doar's network?"

"I don't know him."

The big guy straightened up and went to fetch a straight back chair. He moved it up so close that when he sat in front of Penny their knees were touching.

"There have been some fires in Yaupon Bay," the big guy said. "A church, a community center."

"I read about them."

"Who is setting them?"

Penny flinched back in his seat. "I don't know. Why would I know something like that?"

"Because you associate with racist scum. Why do they come?"

"Who?"

"The people who come to your rallies. Why do they come?"

"To be with people who think like they do, I guess. And to hear the speakers."

"Who can't be known in advance, according to you."

"My rallies have a good reputation, I guess."

"So, they just come and give you money and listen to whoever might show up to give some sort of talk, and they hang around a little and then they go home."

Penny sat silent.

"I don't like the answers I'm getting," the big guy said.

About the next few minutes Slick would have dark dreams for many months. The big guy's hand flicked out and plucked a hair from the side of Penny's head. And then there was a sound. Or if it wasn't exactly a sound, that was the closest word Slick could find for it. He was reminded of wind in treetops, high up and far away.

Penny went rigid in his seat. His eyes popped wide, as if he were seeing something he'd never seen before and wished he hadn't now. The big guy leaned in close, so he was talking right into Penny's ear. Slick could hear the sound of his voice but not the words. Sometimes Penny would nod. Sometimes he'd shake his head. Sometimes he'd say a word or two.

Even when he felt the cold sweat break out, Slick couldn't stop looking.

Finally, the big guy straightened up and pulled back. Penny slumped in his seat. He looked like some inner part of him had gone missing.

Slick noticed that the big guy looked like someone who'd put down a burden.

"He was telling the truth about Rae and the fires," the big guy said to the Fulmen guy. "He doesn't know Rae, doesn't know anything about the fires. He was lying about his rallies and the Doar connection.   He doesn't have a mailing list, but the people do know each other. They operate by word of mouth for the most part, for security. It's almost a Congress of sorts. Representatives of smaller groups all across this end of the state. They meet, share information and plans, pool money. Some of the money covers the rally expense. Some of it goes to Penny for doing the work. Some of it goes to Doar. I expect we'll find Penny's name in Doar's records when we've finished a thorough review."

"Where do we go from here?" the Fulmen guy said.

"Penny is going to convene another rally. If Rae shows up, we'll take him. In any event, we'll take down license numbers and check on the owners."

"We don't' have much time before the eighth."

"Aimee will have to flog the computers hard."

The big guy turned to Slick Hubbard.

"You, too. Get moving. Don't make me unhappy with you."

Slick said to himself that he wouldn't dream of it.

Chapter Sixteen

Facial tics were Willie Rudd's trademark and Number One Curse. His countenance was a jumble of leaping eyebrows and twitching lips.

Willie's Number Two Curse was that he had an eager eye for the ladies, none of whom had anything for him. He was a buck in perpetual rut, but the does always turned away.

He lived therefore in a state of agitated resentment, and resulting friction with his fellow human beings. He was doubly pained by the circumstances of his life, because he felt that deep down, he really was a nice guy. He was sure the world would know him for a very good fellow, if only he could get his ashes hauled once in a while.

When the woman came into the office of Rudd's Storage Plus, Willie's face went into overdrive. She had skin the color of cocoa, black hair falling in waves, a perfect figure, and a smile like sunlight. On top of that, she looked at him like he was the most handsome man in the world.

Willie was so preoccupied that he didn't notice the big man until she introduced the two of them.

"My name is Gloria Mundy. This is my associate, Marcus Lenta."

With one look from the big man, Willie's glimmering fantasies winked out. He returned to his standard mode of agitated resentment -- and to a hunch that things were about to go badly for Willie Rudd.

"What can I do for you?"

"You are Mr. Rudd?"

"Yes."

"We are here to discuss your illegal stockpile of arms and explosives."

"Now wait just a minute. You got something all wrong."

The woman -- her smile now gone -- put a burnished leather briefcase on the counter. From it she extracted an eight by ten photograph. She tapped the photo with a curved forefinger.

"Storage unit number 37. You have rifles and pistols and dynamite and bomb-making chemicals stacked high. You could go to jail for this. And the swastika flag wouldn't help you in court, either."

Willie's face went uncharacteristically slack.

"What the hell? How did you get that?"

"Another colleague broke in and took the photo. Actually, he broke into several units until he found this one. Don't worry. He didn't damage or take anything."

"That stuff's not mine."

"Oh, Mr. Rudd. Come now. Why do I suspect that your customer records will show someone paying an abnormally high rental rate for unit number 37?"

"Customer records are private. And I don't know anything about that stuff there."

The big man circled behind the counter and tapped the keyboard of the office computer.

"Here now," Willie said. "What are you doing?"

"Looking up you customer records," the big man said with another of his looks. "What's the password?"

Willie looked at the floor.

"You can't look at customer records. They're private."

"Don't make me ask again," the big man said in a voice to match the look.

Willie flushed red.

"Nookie," he said.

The big man worked the keyboard and whistled in mock surprise.

"Well, look at what we have here. A man named Doar is paying you a great deal for unit number 37. And here is an inventory of the contents, along with names. Several people have been storing goods in that unit."

"That information is private," Willie said again. "And who the hell are you two, anyway?"

"It's not private anymore," the big man said, as he printed out copies of the inventory for unit 37. "And who are we? We are people who are about to tell you how you are going to live the next several weeks of your life."

"Not cops?"

"No. Worse."

He gestured at an office chair.

"Sit down there."

Willie sat. The big man pulled up another chair and sat before him.

"You've been keeping bad company, Mr. Rudd. People who stockpile the kind of stuff you're keeping here are up to no good. Do you know them well? Talk to them about what they're up to? Are you doing more than keeping their weapons? Are you involved with them personally?"

"No. No. I talk to them some when they come and go. Just chitchat. Hello. How are you. That kind of thing."

"Why should I believe you?"

"It's true. I swear."

"Doar sends them?"

"Yes."

"And you deal with Doar."

"Yes. He pays me to provide the space -- and not to ask questions. Which I wouldn't do anyway. These guys are not the kind you ask questions."

"So, you haven't heard them say anything about a church burning in Yaupon Bay."

"No. Nothing."

"Have you heard them say anything about a man named Dolph Rae?"

"No. I don't hang around near them. They come, I say hello and look the other way until they leave."

"We'll see about that. For now, their names give us what we need to work on."

"I don't want trouble," Willie said. "I'm just trying to make a living here. I don't get involved with stuff."

The big man leaned in.

"Well, you've got trouble, whether you want it or not. Right now, you're wondering how bad it is and how you might be able to get out of it. You're thinking that maybe you could just delete the inventory file from your computer and try to deny knowledge of unit number 37. Or maybe you're thinking that you could delete the computer file and empty the unit. No evidence, no problem. But none of that would work, Mr. Rudd. You can't deny knowledge of unit number 37, because then you'd have to explain this."

The woman handed over another eight by 10 photo.

"That's you, Mr. Rudd, inside the unit, helping another man -- whose name we shall soon know -- carry in boxes that our colleague found to be full of guns. You see, while he was inside the unit, our colleague installed a surveillance camera. It's still there. You haven't noticed it because it's well camouflaged. And my other colleague, here, is hiding a feature inside your software that will let her computer keep an eye on yours. If you tamper with the inventory list, we will know. If you tamper with the surveillance camera, we will know. And if you do any of those things, I will see that you land on a very short road to prison."

"What do you want?" Willie croaked.

"I want you to carry on business as usual, while we explore the identities and activities behind the names on your inventory list. Let them come and go as usual. Keep on taking Doar's money. Change nothing. Don't flinch, don't twitch, don't frown. We will do the rest."

"This is blackmail."

"Yes, it is."

"You could get me killed."

"We will try very hard not to do that."

"And I'm supposed to just trust you -- whoever you are?"

"Do you see that you have a choice?"

"No," Willie said.

And it occurred to him that he had been 100 percent right. Things were going badly for Willie Rudd.

Chapter Seventeen

Doar bristled when Llewellyn showed up.

"That's not necessary," he growled.

"It was sure as hell necessary when I met your errand boy," Ames growled in return.

"That was a serious mistake on his part. I have told him so."

"Fine. My man stays, nonetheless, or I don't talk to you."

"Does he have a name?"

"To you his name is Insurance. And for purposes of conversation in this room, my name is still Smith."

"Pardon?"

"I take it for granted that you have tried to check up on me. I don't know what you may have found, but I do have a high profile if you look in the right places. I have to assume that whatever we say here in your office may be recorded, so for purposes of any recordings, my name is Smith until I say otherwise."

"There are no recordings. You have my word."

"Which for all I know is worth nothing. I came here offering you material help in matters that I believe may be of interest to both of us. So far, you've sent me to a man who threatened me with a goon, and showed me a picture of a room full of guns with a flag and a silly uniform. And now you've called and said you want to talk again. So, here I am. The ball is in your court, Mr. Doar. And I advise you that you'll have to do a lot better from now on than you have so far."

"Let me begin with a confession. I did check on you."

"And any information you found may or may not pertain to me. You'd have to prove a link, and I know how to protect my privacy. In our conversations, until I say otherwise, my name is Smith. Now, skip the tap-dance, Doar, and let's get down to cases. Tell me why I should let you manage more than lunch money in my behalf."

"Alright, I'm ready to give you a deeper look at my interests."

"Who do I have to meet this time?"

"Me," Doar said.

With a remote on his desktop, he lowered a viewing screen and started a wall-mounted projector. Two outlines of the state of North Carolina appeared on the screen. They were covered with red, blue and purple shapes.

"What are we looking at?" Ames said.

"These are state legislative districts. The state Senate is on the top map, the House of Representatives on the bottom map. The red districts are consistently Republican and conservative. The Blue ones are consistently Democratic and more liberal. The purple ones swing back and forth. They are the ones that traditionally have made North Carolina a swing state. As you can see, the red districts outnumber the blue ones. That is a development of recent years. We have been working to change swing districts red. We've funneled money to candidates whose views we like. It's been slow, but it's working. We are on the way to taking over the legislature. In time, I believe, we will."

"Who's 'we'?"

"One step at a time, Mr. Smith. One step at a time. We've had to be gradual. But with an infusion of money -- big money, you insinuate -- we could move more vigorously."

"As you observed when we first spoke, I could make campaign donations directly at party headquarters."

"And as you observed at that time, you might like to back candidates who wouldn't naturally appear in the party mainstream. That's what we've been doing."

"Without being noticed. Without being spotted."

"Yes. We funnel our contributions through intermediaries."

"Where does the money come from?"

"From people with interests similar to yours and mine."

"Is that what buys the guns in the picture?"

"Yes."

"So, you take over the legislature. So, what?"

"So, that's only one step. There is a man. A good man. He shares the views of people like you and me. He would like to run for governor."

"And you would use my money to help him."

"Yes."

"So, if you're successful, you would control the legislature and the governor's mansion."

"Yes, and in time, the courts."

"Judges are elected in North Carolina."

"But in the higher courts, the ones with the real power, if a judge resigns in mid-term, the governor appoints an interim successor who then runs with the advantage of incumbency."

"So," Ames said, "in essence you're planning to take over the whole state."

"Yes. And give it back to the good, hard-working people who built it in the first place."

"Lots of *ifs* in your plan."

Doar clicked the projector off and rocked back in his chair. "Meaning what?" he said.

"If your legislative candidates keep winning. If your governor candidate wins. If the right judges resign. "

"Judges are human beings. They have pasts, families, vulnerabilities. There are ways of persuading human beings to cooperate. As for the elections, we plan to stack the deck."

"How?"

"At the right time, we will introduce a little creative tension."

"Meaning what?"

Doar rose and waddled to the decanters on the sideboard. "Drink?"

"I don't mind."

"One for your man?"

"No."

Doar poured, returned to his desk, handed a double bourbon to Ames.

"Our candidates, including the one for governor, will share a philosophy. Its backbone will be law and order. Get the disrupters off the streets. Support the police. Put the criminals where they belong. Make the Muslims keep their place. At the right time, we will create incidents to make these views especially attractive."

"How?"

"Any number of ways. Shoot up a police car. Plant some explosives at a military base and arrange for them to be discovered. Leave some radical-sounding slogans here and there. Provoke some whining demonstrators into the streets and arrange for things to turn violent. It's not hard to push that sort of thing over the edge."

Ames lumbered up from his chair and moved to the office window. Charlotte's bank towers gleamed in the slanting fall sunlight. The conversation made him want to shower himself clean.

"Guns, explosives, violence," he said, turning back to the room. "That's why you're stockpiling the stuff in Hunter's picture. That's what they are waiting to do. The people who send you money and store the guns."

"Not exactly," Doar said.

"I don't understand."

"Those people are over the hill. Has-beens. I feed their delusions and give them a place to store their toys."

"Why."

"So they'll keep sending me money. And I do suppose we might use them from time to time for some very low-level stuff. But they are amateurs. If their activities attracted too much attention, their toys would be traced. They would be tracked down. We couldn't afford to have that happen."

"And so, how would you make it happen? Your *creative tension*, as you put it."

"We would hire professionals. People whose identities, tools and methods would be untraceable."

"Professional criminals, you mean."

"Exactly."

"And the race war that Hunter talked about?"

"A fantasy that many of my donors like to indulge."

"He said your people were waiting for a signal from someone higher up."

"Part of the fantasy."

"But there is someone higher up."

"You could say that."

"I've heard a name. As I've looked around at my options, I've heard a name. Dolph Rae. Some people seem to see him as a leader. Is he your higher up?"

"Mr. Smith, you do ask premature questions. But that one is easy. No, he's not part of our plans. I've heard of him but I've never met him."

"And you haven't started yet? With the creative tension? With the church burning in Yaupon Bay, for example?"

"No. That doesn't fit our model. We don't want to turn the coloreds into more sympathetic figures than they already enjoy being."

Ames stroked his chin and feigned deliberation. He rose, crossed to the window again, crossed back.

"Who is your man? The one for governor."

"You don't get that name until after you've bought in."

"And so you want my money to buy professional criminal help."

"Yes. If we create the right atmosphere, the campaign contributions will flow naturally."

"And if you're successful, you'll use the entire mechanism of state government to crack down on the whiners and the takers and the slackers and the radicals."

"Precisely. And create a proper climate for hard-working people to build wealth and get ahead."

"How would I go about buying in?"

"I would create an account to hold the funds for hiring our professional help. I would make my own contributions to it. You would write a check made out to that account. Not huge, necessarily, but enough to represent more than casual interest. Afterward you could contribute in cash, if you liked. But for starters I would want your name on a check. Evidence, if you will."

"Evidence of my involvement in a felonious scheme."

"Yes. With that check in hand, our relationship would be quite clear. If you ever betrayed me, I would betray you."

Ames rocked back in his chair and gave Doar a grim smile.

"I will think it over, Mr. Doar. You tell an interesting story, but so far, it's only that. A story. It would still leave me in the position of giving you a sum of money and trusting you not to cheat me."

"At some point, Mr. Smith, you're going to have to do that. That is your risk. My risks should also be clear to you."

"I'll think it over," Ames said. "Give me some time."

"I'll give you the same time you gave me. I'll give you 48 hours."

"Fair enough," Ames said as he rose to leave.

Llewellyn rose with him and crossed to the front edge of Doar's desk. He planted his palms in the center of the desktop, leaned forward and put himself nose-to-nose with Doar, who shrank back. Llewellyn pressed farther in, until Doar's head was jammed against the back of his chair.

Llewellyn held the position for long moments and then said

…

"BOO!"

He wheeled and left Doar blinking with rage and humiliation.

Chapter Eighteen

Brandi the hostess led the three of them to a clutch of upholstered chairs near the Island Club's broad picture window. Kyle the server brought them a round of Aberlour single malt -- one small ice cube each -- and bar-food plates of calamari, crab dip and bacon-wrapped scallops.

"Where's Lew?" Llewellyn asked.

"Up in Charlotte," Ames said. "He has an appointment with that law firm that's been fronting the real-estate buys north of town."

He turned a lingering gaze to the window. A glassy sea offered only a murmur. The horizon faded from view in a misty rain.

"Your talk with Doar was remarkable," Hood said.

"Yes," Ames said.

He paused a beat before he turned away from the view.

"He claims he has access to professional criminals," Hood said.

"Yes," Ames said, "or is confident he can get it."

"He must have some point of contact," Llewellyn said. "He can't just place a want ad. Could they be among the names Larkin and Aimee took from his computer?"

"People like that wouldn't be sending him money," Ames said.

"A list is just a list," Hood said. "Doar could have put anyone and anything on it. Listing his professional contacts there could be a way of camouflaging them. Hiding the association."

"And none of this has gotten us any closer to finding the church burner or Dolph Rae. At least as far as we can tell." Ames speared a scallop. "Aimee is working her computer magic?"

"Yes."

"Precisely what is she looking for?"

"Signs. Hints. A criminal record. A sealed juvenile record. Or a blank."

"A blank?"

"A name without a past or present. A phony identity."

"What is she finding?"

"So far, nothing."

"She's working both lists? Doar's and the one from the storage place?"

"Yes. She started with the storage list. It seemed the likelier one."

"But so far nothing."

"Nothing."

"She's keeping an eye on the federal people as well?"

"Yes."

"How are they doing?"

"They are going through their usual motions, but they are finding nothing. The mayor and several civic leaders are getting impatient. But when they press for answers, the federal people erect their usual barrier."

"They don't comment about ongoing investigations."

"Precisely."

"That white supremacy rally that you and Larkin arranged. Is that going ahead?"

"Yes. This weekend. We will photograph faces and license plates, and we'll add that data to Aimee's work load."

"Time is running on toward November 8," Llewellyn said. "How do you see us proceeding?"

"Well," Hood said. "We now have two lines of inquiry, one of which we didn't expect. This business with Doar and the political takeover is much more serious than his list first appeared. It must be pursued. You two should keep on there."

"The next step would be more than a little tricky," Ames said. "He wants a check from a man who doesn't exist."

"Not a problem. We keep a dummy bank account funded as a contingency for our work. It carries the name we put on your false corporate records with the state. I'll give you a checkbook, and you can proceed."

"And what will you and your people be doing?"

"We will go ahead with the white supremacy rally this weekend. Aimee will keep monitoring the federal investigation, and processing the lists of names. She'll soon finish cross-referencing

Doar's disbursement records with campaign contribution reports. I'd like to look a few of these donors in the eye."

"What do you expect to find?" Llewellyn said.

"I'd like to see if they know the full scope of Doar's plan. I'd like to see if any of them know Dolph Rae. And perhaps I'll lay the groundwork for drying up a few contributions."

Hood rose and shook hands. "I must leave now. Ames, I will deliver the checkbook to your office later today. The two of you please enjoy your drinks. I'll cover your tab on the way out."

When Hood had gone, Ames returned his gaze to the window.

"Why here?" Llewellyn asked.

"Pardon?"

"Why did you want to meet here?"

"I wanted to look at the ocean."

"So, you've called your doctor back?"

"Yes."

"And?"

"All clear. False alarm."

"So why do you look like somebody stole your pony?"

"The experience shook me, Pete."

"Fear will do that."

"It's not just the fear."

"What, then?"

"I did a lot of thinking. Looking back over my life. I didn't care for what I saw."

"Why the hell not?"

"My choices."

"What about them?"

"I scarcely made any. Not any real ones. Considered ones."

"I don't understand."

"I got into the newspaper business because my family owned the local daily. I got married to the wrong woman because people in my circle got married around a certain age, and I felt my time had come. When my marriage failed and my family soured on me, I ran away."

Llewellyn snapped forward in his chair.

"You ran away to a career that is damn near legendary," he said. "Your civil rights reporting for the wire service was groundbreaking stuff. Head and shoulders above anyone else."

Ames snorted and sipped his drink.

"When I ran away, I stopped by happenstance in the right place at the right time. All that history was exploding all around me. Anyone with a conscience could have written those stories."

"Well, you did make one big life decision. You dropped your career and came back here to Yaupon Bay."

"Yes," Ames said. "But I did that out of guilt. Plain old reflex."

He gazed away to the window, paused, turned back.

"Pete," he said, "if anyone asked me about my life, I could tell them what I did, but I'm not sure I could tell them who I am, because I'm not sure I know."

"Where are you headed with all this, my friend?"

"To Lew."

"Go on."

"He has to leave Yaupon Bay. He is comfortable here. Comfortable with me. That's not a good basis for choosing how to spend the next years of his life. But neither is going for the brass ring because it seems glamorous. He has to belly up to the decision to leave, and make it for proper and considered reasons. He has to ask the right questions of himself. You've been over it with him. Who are you as a man? And who do you want to be? If you get the brass ring but it's not what you thought; or if you get it and lose it; or if you never get it at all, who will you be?"

"But you can't tell him all that?"

"No. It would come across as, *Do what I say, not what I did.*"

"So he has to make the decision on his own."

"Or with a little help from the right kind of friend."

"You mean me again."

"Yes, Pete. Double down on your talks with him. Focus him. Be open about what you're up to. Make him think. Help him see."

"OK. Maybe Annie and I could have him over. He likes her, and vice versa. A friendly setting might help."

"Yes. Please."

The two of them relaxed into their chairs and turned toward the window. Lost in their thoughts and the pull of the ocean view, they didn't notice the approach of the tall, ruddy man until he stepped in front of Ames and offered a handshake.

HIs baritone filled the space around them.

"My daddy always said a proper man gives his name and states his business straight out. I'm Abraham Gloster, and I'm wondering what the dickens a man like you is doing with a man like Daniel Doar."

Chapter Nineteen

Abraham Gloster took a pull on his neat triple bourbon -- *bar stock, son; I can't tell the difference* -- and settled into his chair.

"Pardon the ambush. Let me explain myself," he said. "I'm a lecturer up at Charlotte College. A little sociology, a little American history, a little political science. Been doing it for years. Along the way I took an extra interest in the civil rights movement. And out of that I developed a little sideline. Sort of a hobby that doesn't have much to do with teaching. I started keeping tabs on some of the ugly bastards who didn't make it up into the biggest headlines. Putting together files. Watching where they went and what they got up to when the big episodes started to quiet down and some of the national attention faded away. You'll understand what I'm talking about, Mr. Colville. That's right, isn't it? You're Mr. Colville nowadays?"

"Yes," Ames said. "That's the name I use."

"Well, as you know, behind the worst of the big dogs who got the spotlight there were supporting actors. A lot of them never got called out or arrested or anything, much less tried and punished. They had just stayed sort of in the background and stirred the pot and did some of the smaller dirty work that kept the hate simmering. Well, a lot of those are lame or dead by now, of course. But some of them were just pups, so they're still around and still bastards. And even the ones who aren't around had children they taught the hatred to; or there's a second generation of self-grown bastards who have read and heard about the first and like the taste of the hate. Some people really are just bad human beings, gentlemen, and it seems the type is always with us.

"Anyhow, for some years now I've made a sort of hobby of keeping tabs on such folks. Because they do get up to mischief from time to time, you know. Now and then I've been able to help the authorities figure out who was behind some threats or vandalism or violence. And you know, there's always the possibility that one of them will try something big. That fellow Eric Rudolph, for example. He was small fry until he decided to make that big show in Atlanta.

Well, after years of watching that sort, sometimes I can tell if some are getting big notions. Sometimes I can help the authorities know they should put extra eyes on this one or that one.

"So, anyhow, Mr. Colville, you can understand that I knew about you from the old days. And when I saw the pictures of you and your preacher friend here going in and out of Daniel Doar's office, I was more than a little puzzled, let me say. You've put on a pound or two, like all of us, but I knew you right away."

Ames interrupted with a raised hand.

"Excuse me, Professor Gloster … ."

"Oh, not profesor," Gloster snorted. "I never made it up the ladder, because I refused to get my union card. Not professor. I'm just a lecturer."

"Union card?"

"A PhD. The academic caste system is the best labor union you could want. Limits competition for jobs. Short of getting caught in bed with a dog they can't be fired. The teamsters should want to be so strong. Anyhow, I would never play the game. My little rebellion. So, I'm just a lecturer. Always will be."

"OK, Mr. Gloster. But you say you have pictures of me at Doar's office? You use surveillance equipment?"

"Well, that's a bit of a fancy term for it. Here and there we use deer cameras. You can get them at just about any hunting and fishing store."

"We?"

"People help me. Volunteers. I can't pay anybody. Some of them are people who would be targets if some of the bastards got out of hand. Some are just people whose hearts are in the right place. Fellow across the street from Doar's office lets me mount a deer cam in his window. He's a Jewish lawyer. Sees right through Doar. Has no use for him. So, anyway, when I saw the pictures of you and the preacher going in and out at Doar's, I just couldn't figure it. So, I decided I had to get face to face with you and just ask straight out."

"How did you find me here? I mean, I'm not hiding, but it's been a long time."

"Well, I knew you were from Yaupon Bay, so this was the logical place to start. A couple of phone calls and some Google time did the trick. I was heading to drop in at your office, but I saw you driving away, followed you here. So actually, you weren't all that hard to find. And long as we're on the subject, do you mind my asking just why you dropped out and came back here under another name?"

Ames swigged the last of his drink, signaled Kyle for another.

"Well, no, I guess I don't mind your asking. I dropped out because I got tired of being a hit-and-run artist."

"I don't understand."

"You know what those communities were like after a crisis. The fear, the confusion, the upheaval. And then the task of healing. The people who lived in those places faced years of work and struggle to put things together in a new and livable way. Me? I just hopped a plane to the next hot spot. I guess I finally wanted to be a citizen of more than my profession."

"And your last name. Wrightsman. You dropped it and went to using your middle name."

"Yes. Well, the name had some history here in Yaupon Bay that I didn't want to be associated with any more. My dad was not a forward-thinking man. He and I split over civil rights issues. Me and my wife, too, for that matter. And then my dad sold The Advocate to Pole Star. That hasn't always been a good thing for the town. Some of the name thing was just a chemical urge with me, I guess. A yen for a clean break. As I said, I'm not hiding. People here know who I am. But I'm my own man, not my father's boy. I guess you could think of it as civic body language."

"I see. Well, as long as I've come all this way to pry, I may as well pry. What the hell are you and your preacher friend here doing with Daniel Doar? And by the way, reverend, I must say that you do have a varied wardrobe."

Llewellyn grinned and tipped a nod.

"You've heard about the church burning here?" Ames said.

"Yes. Haven't been able to learn anything about it, but I've been trying."

"So have we."

"Does the 'we' include that big black man who was with you here?"

"Yes."

"Mind my asking who he is?"

"No, I don't mind. His name is August Hood. He's an investigator of sorts. He's interested in the church burning for obvious personal reasons. Also, he has access to information that's not public. He learned that the federal people have lost track of an agitator they were keeping an eye on. HIs name is Dolph Rea. They nicknamed him the Gandy Dancer because he does -- or did -- itinerant track labor for the railroads."

"I've run across him," Gloster said. "Didn't know about the Gandy Dancer name, but I've run across Rea's trail a few times."

"Hood wondered if Rea might be behind the church burning in some way, or if he might have gone underground for some other reasons. He wants to find Rea. Asked me to help."

"Because of your connections from the old days."

"Yes."

"And your connections led you to Doar?"

"Yes."

"Why did he agree to talk to you."

"Because I went as a rich right-winger looking for opportunities to invest in the cause. Pete here and his other wardrobe went along to complement the pose -- and to help me out if things went sour."

"Did Doar help you?"

"Not with the church burning or the Gandy Dancer, but he's up to other stuff that we have decided to pursue."

"What is it?"

"He wants to stack the legislature, take over the governorship and pack the courts. He has a plan for it, the beginnings of some financing -- and, he says, access to professional help."

"What kind of professional help?"

"Criminal help. To stir up the kind of trouble that could make right-wing candidates more attractive."

“Holy shit. And meanwhile, you’ve still got Rea and the church burning thing.”

“Yes.”

“Mind if I pitch in? I might be able to help.”

“You mean you know how we could find Rea? Do you know where he is?”

“No. I don’t know where he is. But I did notice that he dropped off the radar several months ago. And I know where his grandmother lives. She has a little place outside Goldsboro.”

Chapter Twenty

The raised deck of Llewellyn's oceanfront home offered a sweeping view of dunes and surf. Gulls wheeled in a steady breeze. Shorebirds pecked in the sand along the tideline.

"October is my favorite month," Llewellyn said. "The tourists are mostly gone. The heat has broken. Sometimes, in the early morning or evening, you can walk the beach and have it all to yourself. Annie loves to walk on the beach. The sand is easier on her feet. And she likes the bird-watching, too. They're migrating now. All kinds of them out there."

He moved burgers and sausages here and there on a gas grill. His apron said, "Kiss the cook and bring him a beer."

Lew Perry relaxed in a lounge chair and watched a flock of pelicans sail in formation overhead.

"What are we having?" he said.

"Burgers with red beans and rice. I do the burgers and andouille sausage on the grill. Annie does the rest inside with her special spices."

"What are they?"

"I don't know. She says if she told me she'd have to kill me."

Lew sipped a beer and considered the irony of having a clergyman for a friend. Papai would approve, up to a point. He would regret Llewellyn's not being a Roman Catholic. Papai never passed judgment, but he did nurse a fear that people outside the True Faith had at least one foot on the straight road to hell. He viewed protestants with a personal brand of loving pity.

Lew thought Pete Llewellyn was a pretty good guy all around. He was down to earth, and kept the religion stuff to himself for the most part, unless you brought it up. If you brought it up, then the subject was fair game.

And if you tried to debate him, you were in for a test and maybe a scolding. Father Pete thought skepticism was OK, if you knew what you were talking about -- which most people didn't, in his estimation. He had little patience for bafflegab, as he called it.

Yes, Father Pete was one of the good guys. And Annie was a joy. She had a quick, mischievous wit and a resolute smile. She would brook nothing remotely approaching pity about her advancing arthritis. If pressed by someone whose good intentions went too far, she would say, *I don't let what I can't have ruin my enjoyment of what I can have.* And then she would pointedly change the subject.

"Good beer," Lew said, gesturing with his glass. "You say it's from up in Wilmington?"

"Yes. Cape Fear Wine and Beer. That's their red ale. They call it Evil Dead Red."

"What's yours?"

"Mine's an IPA from Broomtail brewery. Acerbic Ecstasy."

"Maybe I'll try one of those next."

"Ames said you'd been up to Charlotte?"

"Yes. I went to see the lawyers who are fronting those land buys up north of town."

"How did it go?"

"Like you might imagine. All smiles and thinly veiled condescension.

We're ever so glad to explain a complicated matter to the youngster from the little weekly paper.

That sort of thing."

"Did they tell you anything at all?"

"Oh, they put on quite a show. Three of them sat with me in a fancy conference room. Picture-window view of all those uptown Charlotte office towers. They spread out an architect's rendering of a mixed-use development. They called it North Harbor. Retail, office space, residential condos. It was pretty impressive."

"They told you all that? Told you right out?"

"They asked if we could talk off the record. I said I'd promise not to make direct use of anything they gave me, but that I would insist on continuing to pursue the story through other sources if I could."

"And they bought it?"

"They didn't like it. Made a show of conferring over it. Then they said they'd take the risk because they wanted to help me understand what I was tampering with. That was a word they used a lot with me. *Tampering.*"

"How so?"

"Well, a project like that needs a lot of land. They haven't finished buying what they need. They argue that premature publicity could drive up the land prices and compromise the project."

"Sounds fishy to me. A project that size has got to have a lot of backing."

"That's what I said. They said to think about the scale of the thing. If you're putting ten million dollars through a funnel, and you save ten cents on the dollar, you've saved a million bucks."

"Ten million?"

"Just a figure for illustrative purposes, they said, to make the arithmetic simple. The real figure could be a lot higher. Or so they hinted."

"So, if you are able to publish a story, you could be hurting a nice piece of economic development for the town."

"Yes. But if I don't publish a story, I'm helping the developer lowball those landowners on a fair price for their land."

"Rock and a hard place."

"Yes. And I don't mind telling you, I don't like having this kind of power over things."

"But you can't escape making a decision, one way or the other."

"No, I can't."

"Comes with the territory, Lew. If you're going to be a journalist, you'll face hundreds of decisions like that."

"So Ames keeps telling me."

"You going to pursue the story?"

"Yes. That's what we do, I guess."

"Where will you look? Zoning applications? Permit applications?"

"Yes. But I may not find anything. It seems early in the project for that. And the developer can afford to take some regulatory risk. If he puts all that land together into one parcel, it will be worth more than the sum of the individual pieces. He can just flip the land if he has to."

"And so, what then?"

"I don't know. I'm still chewing on it."

Annie Llewellyn opened a sliding glass door and called. "I'm ready, grillmeister, if you are."

"Coming right in," Llewellyn said.

They sat around a dinette table. Llewellyn said a brief blessing, and Annie began passing dishes.

"Well, Lew," she said. "I haven't seen you in a while. How are things? You gettin' any?"

"Pardon? Getting What?"

"Lovin'. Sugar in your bowl. Young man like you shouldn't waste his prime. You dating anybody in particular?"

He flashed her a grin. "Does the congregation know the preacher's wife talks like that?"

"Hey, sport, when the Bible lists all those *begats,* it ain't talking about parthenogenesis."

"What's that?"

"Reproduction without sex."

"That would be a bummer for sure. And no, nobody in particular. A couple of girls. Nothing serious."

"Better get a wiggle on. You won't last forever, you know."

Across the table, Peter Llewellyn struggled with a chuckle.

Lew put down his fork and folded his hands in his lap. "Have I told you about my dad?" he said.

"A little," Peter Llewellyn said. "You said he's a finish carpenter in a boatyard up in Rhode Island that builds yachts."

"That's what he does. It's not who he is."

Peter Llewellyn did a double-take.

"You see, I do listen when you and Ames talk to me about that. And you're not the first. My dad says the same kind of things.

Your job is not you. Be careful to know yourself. Figure out what kind of man you are -- and what kind you want to be.

That sort of thing."

"Your dad sounds like a wise man."

"He is. That and more. Let me tell you about him. About his identity. He is a husband, a father, and a child of God. Oh, and Portuguese. He is proud of his American citizenship, but culturally he is Portuguese. I think the only thing I ever did that may have hurt him a bit was to anglicize my name.

" He says America is a tapestry, and each of us sews a bit of himself into it. We give America the gift of ourselves, he said, and that makes it a country like no other. I remember one day when I was a kid -- about ten, maybe -- and he came home from work all excited and he called out to us.

You know what I did on my lunch hour today? I taught a Swede to play sueca. That's America.

"So anyway, he is a husband, even though my Mom passed away. *He says, Oh I know she's gone, and I've moved on, I really have. But becoming a husband is a little like becoming a priest. Once you take the vow and live the life, you become a different person. The old you is gone. I don't live the married life anymore, but I did for a long time, and I became a different person. The old bachelor me, who had never shared his life, is gone. I am the new me that I became.*

He's a husband, and a father -- a damn good one, I say. And he's a child of God. He goes to mass every Sunday, and volunteers in service to the poor, and loves his neighbor. He genuinely loves his neighbor. He's the most non-judgmental man I ever met. I don't have much use for the church, as you know, Pete, but I know a good human being when I see one. My dad has the best spirit of the Christian gospels in the marrow of his bones. So, he's all those things, and he's a walking repository of old country culture. And in just these ways, he is complete. He lives in that little Portuguese enclave where he was born. He has never gone as much as fifty miles from it. He knows who he is, and he's content with it.

"And I know one more thing, folks. That's not me. I'm not the same man as my father, and I never will be. And this is not me, either. Yaupon Bay and The Sand Dollar."

Peter Llewellyn folded his napkin and placed it beside his plate. "You've decided to leave."

"Yes, I have. I may not know who I am, yet, but I know who I'm not."

"Do you know why you've decided to leave?"

"Yes. Because I have to try. That's how I'll find out who I am. For me, finding out who I am means taking the chance of having to face up to who I'm not. If I get the brass ring, as you put it, and it's not what I imagined, then I'll know who I'm not. If I try and try but realize one day that I'll never make it, then I'll know who I'm not. I have to try. The man who doesn't try -- that's not me."

"Sounds like you've made a sound decision," Peter Llewellyn said.

"I hope so. And it is a decision, not a reflex. You and Ames and my dad have taught me to think about the difference. You have taught me how to focus and ask myself at each step of life, *Why am I doing this?*

Peter Llewellyn reached across the corner of the table, put his hand on Lew's shoulder and said, "Then good luck and Godspeed."

"You think Ames will be OK with it?"

"I'm sure he will. He wants you to do what's best for you."

The three of them were so deep in the moment that they didn't notice Clyde Hunter's skinhead goon until he stepped from the deck into the room and leveled a chrome-plated Saturday night special.

"Move away from the table," he said. "Over there. Sit by the wall."

Annie raised her two arthritic hands, which she had flexed into rigid claws. "Can't. She said. "Not without my wheelchair."

"Where is it?" the goon said.

"Down the hall. In the bedroom."

"Forget it. Sit where you are and be quiet. You other two. Go over and sit on the sofa by the wall."

The goon fetched a dinette table chair and placed it so that all three of them were in his field of vision.

"You." he said to Peter Llewellyn. "You made me look bad in front of my boss. I don't like that. Ain't gonna take it. So I took down your license number along with the old guy's. Tracked you down and found out you're some kind of preacher. That made me real curious, so I tracked down the home address the old guy gave with the car rental.

" Went there saying I had a package to deliver. Old lady who answered the door said she never heard of the old guy. So, you're not who you pretended to be, and the old guy is not who he pretended to be, and I'm gonna look better with my boss when I find out the truth and serve you up to him. "

The goon leaned forward and focused a glare on Peter Llewellyn.

"Start talking, preacher man."

The goon was startled when Annie called out, and lost a part of his concentration.

"Hey asshole," she shouted.

"What?" he said, turning.

"About the wheelchair? I lied."

And she held him in one more moment of distraction by rising and doing a neat two-step beside the dinette table.

Peter Llewellyn took advantage of the opportunity and landed on the goon's right ear a looping haymaker that knocked him off his chair. The Saturday night special flew from his hand and slid to a stop between Annie's feet. She scooped it up and leveled it in a two-handed grip.

The goon broke into a sly grin.

"You gonna shoot me, preacher's wife? I don't think so."

He dove through the door, vaulted the deck rail and sprinted away.

Annie put the gun on the table, sank into her chair and buried her face in her hands. Lew leaned back on the sofa and mopped his brow.

"We have to call the police," he said.

"Not much point," Llewellyn said. "He'll have an alibi provided to him by a retired law officer."

"Then what do we do?"

"The first thing is we tell Ames that his whole deal has been blown, and he's now going to be targeted by a man who says he has professional help at his disposal. They can find him, if they try hard enough. He's likely to be in serious danger."

"Us, too," Annie said, looking up. "We're in danger, too."

"Yes," Peter Llewellyn said. "I'm afraid so."

Chapter Twenty-One

They took The Highway to U.S. 17 north, picked up I-40 West at Wilmington, headed up U.S. 117 toward Goldsboro. Ames led the way in a sedan rented under another false identity. After the incident at the Llewellyns', he didn't want his own license plates to be seen.

Larkin and Gloster followed in Larkin's black Mercedes. They had arranged particulars to offer the least alarm to Adelaide Rea. Ames would go to the door alone. If he then needed help, or simply wanted to invite them in, he would signal on a pocketed cell phone with Larkin's phone set on speed dial.

"There are five logical possibilities," Larkin said. "The grandmother is there alone; she is there with others; Rae is there with her; Rea is there with her and others; Rea is there alone.

"As long as circumstances permit, Ames will play the role of the wealthy benefactor. He's heard of Rea's leadership at rallies. He is interested in the same sorts of issues. He wants to inquire about teaming up with Rea to advance the cause."

Gloster watched the sandy flats of eastern North Carolina slide by. "And if Rea is there alone?"

"We will take him with us," Larkin said.

Gloster swiveled away from his view of the passing countryside. "He is unlikely to be agreeable to that."

"We will persuade him," Larkin said. He used his left hand to pull his coat open and reveal a nine-millimeter pistol nestled in his armpit.

"You'd force him?"

"We would kidnap him, yes."

"That's dangerous as hell. You would have to free him eventually."

"Yes."

"He would report it to the authorities."

"That would be a very awkward undertaking for a man who's been hiding from the authorities for six months.

Officer, I'm Dolph Rea. I've been in hiding, but I've come out now to report that I was kidnapped and held against my will by two old men and a little black guy. Why? Oh, well, never mind that part. A white supremacist? Yes, I guess you could say that about me. Why have I been hiding? What have I been doing? Do I know anything about the arson in Yaupon Bay? No, no. Look, let's just skip it. They didn't hurt me or anything."

"I see," Gloster said, turning back to the view.

"How did you find her?" Larkin said. "The grandmother."

"Quite by accident. We had run across Rea's trail a few times, but we couldn't pin him down or learn much about him. He was always on the move.

" I put out word on our network. Asked all our helpers to be alert for any sign of him. One of them runs a little grocery market in the Goldsboro area. He delivers groceries to Adelaide Rea. A couple of times she ordered extra -- things she never had ordered for herself. Our man kidded her about sneaking a man into her house. She said she was expecting a visit from her grandson. Our man teased the name out of her. Dolph."

"But you still weren't able to pin him down."

"No. He only came a couple of times, near as we can tell. Came at night, left early the next day. By the time our folks were able to get to the neighborhood, there was no sign of anyone being there with her."

"What do you know about her? I mean, is she likely to be cooperative? Does she share his views?"

"We don't know much. The little we've learned came through gossip at our man's store. It's that kind of place. A community crossroads. People hang out there, chew the fat. Our man overhears things. And of course he chats with the grandmother himself.

"She is widowed. Has been for a long time. Rea's father was her only child. He left home young, seldom came back. We don't know when or why the boy reconnected with his grandmother. We aren't sure if she shares his view. Guesswork says not. Our man

and the cracker-barrel bunch at his store haven't heard her say
anything about issues of any sort. She's quite gentle, they say.
Lives quietly, has a few lady friends about her age. Seems to dote
on the boy. Our man says she lit up when she talked about him."

They left the Interstate and turned up the last leg on U.S.
117.

"Where is your colleague? Hood." Gloster said.

"He went to Charlotte to see Daniel Doar."

"Doar agreed to see him?"

"No. Doar will be very surprised. Hood wants to put a stop to
his grand scheme. And for starters he wants to persuade Doar that
it would be a very bad idea to hunt Ames and the Llewellyns."

"Sound like a pretty tall order."

"Hood can be very persuasive," Larkin said with a tiny smile.

"Ames and the Llewellyns have moved out of harm's way, I
guess, for the time being?"

"Yes. Ames has moved in with us. Annie Llewellyn has
moved in with a friend. Father Pete has moved in with Lew Perry.
They are personal friends. They race a sailboat together."

"But Hunter's man saw Perry. He was there at the
Llewellyn's house."

"Yes. But he doesn't know who Lew is."

"Yes. I see."

"Ames and Annie should be fine," Larkin said. "But the priest
is going to be a problem."

"How so?"

"He has promised to stay out of sight during the week, but he
refuses to give up conducting Sunday services."

"How will you deal with that?" Gloster said.

"I'll be his bodyguard," Larkin said, lifting his coat to show the
pistol again.

They left the highway for a winding country lane. Adelaide
Rea lived in a clapboard bungalow. Her neatly tended front yard
was marked off by a low, white picket fence. A 20-year-old Chevy
sedan sat in a side carport. Ames pulled into her sandy driveway.
Larkin drove on just out of sight, then turned around and parked on
the shoulder to wait.

"Your man Hood." Gloster said. "Why does he do this? Get involved in this kind of thing?"

"Why do you ask?"

"He has money?"

"Yes."

"He doesn't have to get involved?"

"No."

"Then why?"

"Because he cares about it. Pretty much the same reason you do what you do, I'm thinking."

"A few minutes ago, when you said he can be very persuasive. You said it as though you meant something in particular by it."

"Yes."

"What was it?"

"Before this is over, you're likely to see for yourself."

Larkin's phone buzzed and he reached to answer.

"Yes. You all right? Oh. I see. Yes, we'll be right there."

"Is she there?" Gloster said.

"Yes."

"Alone?"

"Yes."

"Is she cooperating?"

"No. She's dead."

The house was a throwback to decor of yesteryear -- flower prints, white doilies and linoleum floors. Adelaide Rea was slumped at a kitchen table with a deck of cards scattered before her.

"Apparently she died playing solitaire," Ames said. "No sign of anything beyond natural causes. No one else in the house. No sign that anyone else has been here recently."

"Damn." Gloster said. "We've hit a wall."

"Not necessarily," Larkin said. "We'll search the house. There may be traces of the grandson somewhere."

The search revealed that Adelaide Rea was the soul of neatness and simple living.
Closets were models of order. Beds were carefully made. Kitchen supplies and tools were stored, each in an appointed place. A desk

contained records of a checking account; Social Security check stubs; a schedule of services and meetings at a nearby church; stationery and a fountain pen.

The checkbook records showed only ordinary bill payments. The stationery drawer showed no sign of correspondence to or from anyone. Car keys hung on a peg by the front door. The car was empty except for registration papers in the glove compartment.

They searched and then searched again. After an hour of effort, they had found only a list of telephone numbers beside a landline set in the main hallway.

"Looks like this is all we're going to get," Larkin said, scanning the list. "Just numbers and initials. No names. More work for Aimee."

"What are we going to do about the grandmother?" Ames said. "We can't just leave her here. But how can we report it. How would we explain being in the house?"

"I'll call our man the grocer," Gloster said. "Tell him to put together another delivery for her today. He'll be the one who finds her. He'll do it. He'll understand."

Larkin's cell phone buzzed.

"Hello? Yes, Hood, we found her, but she's dead. No. Natural causes. We searched the house but only came up with a list of phone numbers with initials. I'll get that to Aimee right away. Should be short work for her. He's gone? That's a complication. Yes. Yes. All right, we'll meet at home."

"What happened?" Ames said.

"Doar's office says he's away on business, and there's no one at his home. Hood is going to stay in Charlotte and watch the house tonight. And there's been another fire and another note from Omega.

A dumpster behind the Rosa Parks elementary school. It was rigged with some sort of motion or gravity-activated device. When the truck inverted the dumpster to empty it, the thing went up and the truck went with it. The driver was lucky to get away alive."

"What did the note say?"

" 'Still here, Lilliputians. Tick, tick, tick.' "

"Damn," Ames said.

Chapter Twenty-Two

In Larkin's Mercedes they had Hood on speaker phone.

"Is it convenient for you to fill me in?" Hood said.

"Yes, Larkin said. "Aimee did indeed make short work of the phone numbers from the grandmother's house. All but one were ordinary -- doctor, dentist, church, grocery store, next door neighbor. That sort of thing. Only one stood out. It traced to a Bethany Scott in Wilmington.

"Could be camouflage," Hood said.

"Maybe. But when I called it, a woman answered. I said I'd called a wrong number. The property is a rental. I elected not to call the owner. Didn't want to set off alarms if Rea is there."

"I agree. How are you going to handle it?"

"Similar to yesterday. Going in cold. Ames is ahead, and will go alone at first. If Rea is not there, he'll pose again as a would-be benefactor. If Rea is there, we'll have to tell him that his grandmother just died, and then play it from there."

"Hunter intimated that Doar is not at the top of the food chain in his scheme. A higher-up could be the gubernatorial candidate, or someone close to him. Or it could be Rea."

"Yes. We will be very careful. How about you? Have you made any progress?"

"No, not really. I've had a camera on his house all day. Did some homework on the campaign contribution intermediaries while I waited. There's been no movement. I tried his office again this afternoon. They say he's still away. Won't say anything more."

"What do you think is going on?"

"It could be just as they say -- a routine business trip."

"And if it's not?"

"Doar surely knows by now that his scheme has been compromised and that Hunter's thug botched the visit to the Llewellyns. The thug wouldn't have risked keeping it from Doar, because he doesn't know who Ames is or what he may do next. Doar may have gone to ground, to keep Ames from coming at him from an unexpected direction. If Doar really does answer to a higher-up, he'll want to get the situation remedied quickly. He won't want any appearance that he can't keep things under control. He'll be intent on finding Ames and Llewellyn, and dealing with them."

"Which means Llewellyn is a prime target."

"Yes. You must stay very close to him."

"I've made all the arrangements he'll tolerate. What will you do now?"

"I can't spend any more time just waiting. Doar told Ames that he has an account from which he pays the expenses of his operation. You found no record of that in his office. Only the ledger entries on the computer. If I can find the account records, I may be able to find Doar. I'll go back to his house in a few hours. If the camera still shows no movement, I'll break in and search. Also, I've identified a couple of big givers among the intermediaries. I plan to visit them and question them in detail about how they receive the money they're laundering."

"Good hunting. We'll check in later, after we've made our visit."

"Yes," Hood said, and the line went dead.

With a setting sun in their rear-view mirror, they passed the battleship North Carolina, crossed the Cape Fear River, and made their way to a neighborhood of modest brick ranch houses. When they reached their target, Larkin and Gloster stopped down the block. Ames pulled up in front. He paused in his rented car for a few moments, wondering if he might soon be assaulted or shot.

"Well, no guts no glory," he murmured, and climbed from the car.

The doorbell was answered by a young African-American woman in running shoes, jeans and a chambray shirt.

Ames swallowed his surprise and said, "Hello, I am acting in behalf of the family of Adelaide Rea. Your phone number was found among her belongings. Are you acquainted with her?"

The young woman's brow furrowed with worry and curiosity. "Of course I know her. She's Dolph's grandmother."

"Dolph Rea? Do you happen to know where he is? His family would want me to reach him."

"Yes, I know where he is." She jerked a thumb over her shoulder. "He's in the kitchen. We were just cleaning up after dinner."

"Beth?" a man called out from within the house. "Everything OK?"

A trim young man appeared, drying his hands on a dish towel. He was the very image of the Dolph Rea photos, except that his eyes were not vacant.

Chapter Twenty-Three

"Sad but not completely surprising," Rea said as he touched the corner of one eye with the back of a forefinger. "She was failing. We both knew it. I stayed in touch, helped as I could. But her body was just wearing out."

"It appeared she went peacefully," Ames said. "As though she just decided it was time to stop playing cards."

Rea tipped a silent nod and stared into a far corner.

"Does she have any other living relatives?" Ames said.

Rea shook his head. "No, just me. I guess I'll have some details to handle."

He blinked himself awake from memories. "Tell me again, if you would, why you were Looking for her? For me?

"There have been some arson fires in the black community of Yaupon Bay."

"Yes. I've read about them."

"I work with an investigator who has taken a personal interest. He learned that you had suddenly dropped out of sight. The authorities were concerned about the possible reasons. And about the fact that you were last seen near Yaupon Bay. My associate wondered if you might be involved with the arsons in some way, or at least have some information about them. He set out to find you, asked me and some others to help."

He gestured at Larkin and Gloster.

"Because of my past," Rea said. "The things I associated myself with."

"Yes," Ames said. "We wanted to find you because we thought you might know something -- or someone. But I must tell you candidly we never expected to find anything like this."

He gestured at Rea and Bethany Scott, both of whom smiled.

"I'm on the faculty at UNC Wilmington," she said.

"Sociology. I was doing a project on

the psychology of racism. I ran across accounts of Dolph's appearances at rallies. I was intrigued. He was ever so articulate. And ever so misguided. I couldn't figure it out. Couldn't put the two together."

Rea took her hand.

"It was about a year ago," he said. "She got a white friend to attend one of the rallies. He followed me afterward to the apartment I was using at the time. One day she just showed up at the door. She didn't even say hello. Just stuck out her hand and said, *I'm Beth and I would like to learn to understand you.*"

Bethany Scott put her free hand atop his.

"She wasn't afraid or hostile. Now, in the world I had known, everybody was afraid or hostile or both. I had never seen anybody like her. Never imagined it. Might as well have been a Martian standing at my door. So, I invited her in. Didn't know why at the time. Just natural curiosity, I guess. She settled right down, and we had a beer and started talking. Pretty soon I realized she loved books as much as I did. And she had read so many of the ones I liked. She had read them, but she didn't see them the same way. And she knew a lot more than I did about context. Why the books were written. Who the intended audience was.

"Well, I was fascinated. So, she came back again, and then again, and pretty soon we got to sitting down quite regularly to read and talk and debate. Oh, boy, did we debate. And she never judged. She met me where I was, and helped me see why she was over where she was, and I felt like I was being fed.

"After a while, when we kind of wound down from talking about books and such, we'd get on to some more personal stuff. Background, family. I told her about what it was like when I was a kid. Got some stuff off my chest that I'd never said out loud before. And once again she didn't judge or comment. Just listened and listened. One night -- there was a moon -- we were out for a walk talking about that kind of stuff, and we wound up holding hands. And I said, *I'm different than I was.* And she said, *No you're not. You're just seeing parts of yourself you never looked at before. They were always there.* And I said, *I've had girlfriends before, but never a partner. Never like this.* And she said, *Me too. Only not girlfriends of course. Boyfriends. Oh, you know what I mean.* And we laughed, and I turned my back on the life I'd been living, and we've been together ever since."

"Quite a change," Ames said. "But I do have to ask you some questions."

"Fire away."

"Do you know a man named Daniel Doar?"

"I've heard of him. He courts various kinds of right-wing interests, I guess. But I've never met him. Why are you interested in him?"

"We stumbled across him when we were trying to develop some leads on who might be behind the fires."

"Do you think he is?"

"Probably not. But he claims to be organizing a right-wing political movement. It could be pretty bad. He works with a man named Clyde Hunter. Know him?"

"Never heard of him."

"On a different note: Slick Hubbard? Marvin Penny?"

"Yes. Rally organizers. I know who they are, but I am not really acquainted with them. Only saw them once or twice."

"Do you know about stockpiling of weapons and explosives in Fayetteville?"

Rea paled. "No. Nothing. Look, let's be clear. Back in the day, I was mostly mouth. I fancied myself a kind of philosopher of the common people. I was never actually involved in anything. Just went to events where the crowd was likely to be cordial, did my thing and moved on."

"Then why did you drop out of sight? Why did you hide?"

Rea craned forward, put his elbows on his knees, fixed Ames with a long look. "Think about it," he said. "Do you know what could happen to us if the people I used to associate with found out about Beth and me? I've got an opportunity, but I've also got a problem. The opportunity is that I can have a whole new life. The problem is that, in that life, I can never take the risk of being me again. I have to become a whole new person. And the first very specific instance of that problem is that it severely complicates our intention to be married. So, while we try to figure some things out, I lie low and work odd jobs and live here with Beth."

"And you know nothing about the fires in Yaupon Bay? Not even some hunches that might be helpful?"

"No. I'm just not equipped to help you there."

"Because you've been out of circulation for most of a year?"

"No. Because you're barking up the wrong tree."

"What?"

"The fires are not motivated by racism."

Larkin's head snapped up. "What do you mean?" he said.

"Omega has been signaling that in his notes. Unintentionally, perhaps, but he's been signaling. A racist arsonist wouldn't use all those obscure literary references. He'd be crowing in plain language about the superiority of the white race. Omega tipped you off in the very first note. He said he was the one who'd burned the *black* church."

Ames, Larkin and Gloster questioned with their eyes.

"The kind of man you're looking for would not have called it that. He would never have said *black*. He would have used the ugliest racial epithet he could think of. The arsons aren't racial hate crimes. The racial angle is a feint."

Larkin buried his face in his hands. "Oh my God, he's right. I should have seen it immediately. We've wasted half the time of the warning he gave us."

Chapter Twenty-Four

On the screened deck that spanned the back side of the Hoods' house, Bethany Scott settled into a wicker armchair beside Abraham Gloster.

"What do you think, Mr. Gloster? Should I interview you for my project on the psychology of racism?"

"Well, Ma'am, I'd be glad to try to help you, but I'm not sure how useful I'd be. For starters, I'm a simple-minded man. I have a very limited appetite for psychology. To me, a psychologist is one goldfish persuading the rest that he can see all of them from outside the bowl.

"Now, about racism, I could tell you some things. And if I were to try to cover all of them, we might be here until Christmas. If I were to choose just one thing to tell you, I'd say remember not to lose sight of first principles. Yes, it's good to be respectful of different approaches to problems and to different ideas about solutions. To try to understand before we presume to condemn. But there can be extremes even in that. My daddy used to say *Abe, it's good to be open to different points of view. But don't get so open-minded that your brains fall out.* Keep an eye on cold fact, Ms. Scott. On first principles."

"And first principles are … ?"

"There is such a thing as evil in the world. And some people are just vicious bastards. And that's all there is to it. Yes, it's important to try to distinguish between the vicious bastards from the rest. But it's also important to identify a vicious bastard when you see one. To name him for what he is."

"Dolph is not a vicious bastard."

"No, I can see that he is not."

"He was reared in a certain way. People speak with the accent of their upbringing, and the vocabulary. And they understand the world as it is portrayed to them by the people who are rearing them. He was brought up to be afraid, and to be angry about being afraid, and to always be poised to strike the first blow."

"Yes," Gloster said. "Sadly, there are many like him. But also sadly, there are many who should be viewed only through first principles. They are everywhere, and they are always with us."

At the foot of the deck stairs, a mahogany runabout sat at a floating dock. A tidal creek wound away through the swamp. Midday sunlight fell through a ribbon of space between the treetops along the bank. Parts of the creek sparkled. Parts were black in the deep shade of the swamp.

"The Barren is beautiful in a mysterious kind of way," Bethany Scott said.

"Yes. And a dangerous way, too. Danger is fascinating -- if you don't actually have to face it. I like our safe distance here."

"That was some lunch, Mr. Gloster. Vegetables, fish, beef. You must have been grilling out here for hours."

"It's my element. You want to make me complete, give me a grill and a bottle of bourbon and stand back."

Lew Perry stepped up behind them. "They are ready inside," he said.

They went to the open living room and settled with the rest of the group in a circle of leather easy chairs. Hood signaled for attention.

"We're on a very short fuse with the arson fires," he said. "Let's start with that. A feint suggests and order of calculation we hadn't considered. And a range of possibilities that poses a serious challenge. It could be premeditated mass murder. A catch-me-if-you can kind of thing. Or arson for hire. Revenge. Or fraud. This Omega could strike anywhere for any of a lot of reasons. Aimee, what do the local authorities say?"

"They're skeptical of a feint. They still think it's racial."

"And the federal people?"

"Skeptical."

"And Greenlee and the clergy association? Their citizen surveillance effort?"

"Skeptical."

Hood looked a silent question at Dolph Rea.

"I guarantee it," Rea said. "The vocabulary is wrong, the behavior is wrong, the body language of the whole thing is wrong. These are not racial hate crimes."

"We've lost important time focusing on a racial angle in the arson fires. We need all the help we can get. Ames, I suggest that you and Father Llewellyn take Mr. Rea to see the mayor and his people. Maybe a face-to-face with him well help them see. Also, a visit with Greenlee and the surveillance people might be good. Larkin, if you wouldn't mind going along? I think it wise for you to stick very close to Ames and Father Llewellyn for the foreseeable future."

The four nodded agreement.

"What about the federal people?" Lew Perry asked.

"They won't listen," Hood said. "Not a good use of our time. Aimee, I'm afraid we have to ask even more of you and your computers. We'll need a significantly widened inquiry across jurisdictional lines from, say, Virginia across the two Carolinas, Georgia and Alabama."

"Yes," Aimee said. "We'll need to check arson crimes solved and unsolved. Also, white collar and financial crimes of various sorts. Insurance fraud, business failure scams, that sort of thing. We'll be hacking into law enforcement systems, insurance investigation files. This is going to be a big undertaking."

"I can help if you like," Bethany Scott said. "I do a lot of data massage in my work. I'm more than computer literate. If you can gain me access to the information, I can help with analysis."

"That would be good, thanks." Aimee said.

"Well then," Hood said. "On to Doar and his scheme."

"I found something in the files from the Fayetteville storage business," Aimee said. "A blank name. A name with no discoverable past, and darned few current life details."

"And it is?"

"Jesse Hoyt. The federal authorities have it listed as a known alias."

"For whom.?"

"Extra problem there. They don't know. The name is associated with incidents ranging from armed robbery to kidnapping to murder. Yes, arson, too. Sometimes it appears to have been used by a man, sometimes by a woman. Physical descriptions vary. It could be an identity for rent by anyone with enough money."

"So," Hood murmured. "Doar really does have access to major league muscle. Any twitches on our Fayetteville surveillance systems?"

"No," Aimee said, "and we're not likely to get any that are worthwhile. For a person of that sort, guarding against surveillance would be second nature. He -- or she -- would know how to come and go without giving us any good looks."

"We must be very careful. Father Llewellyn, I believe you should move out of Mr. Perry's place and take a room with us here. Your wife should come, too. We have bed clothes and toiletries for you to use tonight. We'll make arrangements for you to gather other belongings tomorrow. And about the Sunday services, is there any possibility you could change your mind?"

"No," Llewellyn said.

"Please. You take vacations, you travel to meetings, you get sick."

"I might hand the service over to my assistant for any number of reasons. But not out of fear and cowardice. Besides, you know that the Doar people will look at the Sunday service as a venue for getting to me. I won't leave my staff and congregation alone in the crosshairs, and I won't cancel worship altogether."

Hood turned to Annie. "Mrs. Llewellyn?"

"No," she said. "He won't do it, and I would never ask him to."

"Very well. Sunday will be a special challenge. We will work on it. And we will work on baiting Doar and his people into the open. We don't want simply to sit and wait for their next move to appear. When I searched Doar's house, I found nothing. Items of personal life only. This I think suggests that his secret business proceeds through a third location. He told Ames there was a bank account through which his funds were moved. With a bank account there would be balance and transaction records. There were none in his home and none in his office. Only the ledger on his computer. Also, the ledger suggests a relatively high volume of paperwork associated with the account. Money in, money out to the intermediaries. And they of course would be expecting it. The checks would not simply arrive out of the blue, with an expectation that they would divine what to do with them. There would have to be prior communication. Correspondence of some sort. A third location and a material volume of transactional activity suggests the possibility of an aide, a helper, an assistant of some sort, possibly even someone with authority to access funds. If we find the account, we may find the location. If we find the location, we may find the aide. And if we find the aide, we have a hostage hold on Doar."

Ames rose and lumbered to a sideboard of beverages. He held up a bottle of Buffalo Trace, gestured at Gloster and questioned with his eyebrows. Gloster grinned and nodded.

"And how do we go about all this?" Ames said.

"Several ways," Hood said. "For starters, we find out where the first checks are sent. The contributions from Doar's supporters. Ames, can you get back in touch with your original contact and ask them to help you find out where contributions are sent?"

"Glad to."

"Could I ride along?" Lew Perry said. "We could catch up."

"Good idea."

"I will tackle the other end of the money trail," Hood said. "I will identify a couple of big donors and press them on the source of their funds. With luck I'll be able to see a copy of the checks they receive from Doar. On my way, I'll check on Clyde Hunter. I'm sure he's gone to ground, too. Doar wouldn't leave him exposed. But I'll check."

Larkin leaned into the circle. "And what about this Hoyt person? How do we tackle that one?"

"You go to Fayetteville and steal his stash. Clean that unit out."

"You're thinking the man at the storage unit will report it," Lew Perry said.

"Not to the police, certainly. And it's not likely he knows how to reach Hoyt and Doar. Not now, at any rate. They would not let themselves be vulnerable to an underling of that sort. We will send

Doar a message. He'll have to stay at least occasionally in touch with his law office. Larkin, you can break in and leave a message informing him that we've emptied the Fayetteville property. Make it dramatic. Write it on a wall, perhaps. His staff will tell him, even if they don't understand what it means. When you rob the Fayetteville site, use a vehicle traceable to a location we can watch. The storage business' regular parking lot surveillance cameras will pick it up."

Aimee rose from her chair and gestured at Bethany Scott. "If that's all we have for me at the moment," she said, "I think that Bethany and I might go to the computer room and get started. We have a lot of work ahead of us."

"Yes," Hood said. "That's a good idea."

He turned to Lew Perry. "Mr. Perry, how close are you to wrapping up the next edition of The Sand Dollar?"

"I put it to bed tomorrow."

"And on the edition after that, can you work remotely? Away from the office?"

"For the first few days, yes. Why do you ask?"

"I want to suggest that you put Ames' picture in the edition you're closing tomorrow. For a time after that, it won't be safe for you to be in the newspaper office alone."

Lew shot a look at Ames, who tipped a nod.

"Glad to help," Lew said.

"What about his house?" Rea said.

"I live above the office," Ames said.

Hood turned to Abraham Gloster.

"Mr. Gloster, it's possible we'll have to keep an eye on several locations for a time. Do you think we could tap your network of volunteers to help with that?"

"Absolutely. I'll get right on it."

Hood turned to Dolph Rea.

"Mr. Rea, you are among friends here. Do you mind if I raise a personal matter with you?"

"No," Rea said. "I guess not."

"My wife, my father-in-law and I are consultants of a sort. We help people solve problems for a fee. Your problem is that you would like to begin a new life with Ms. Scott, but your past and your previous associations represent a serious hindrance, even a threat to your safety. We can help you solve that problem. We can provide you with a completely new identity from birth onward. It would be unbreakable. If you were to make some cosmetic changes in your appearance, you and Ms. Scott could go on to lead any life you chose."

Bethany Scott took Rea's hand in both of hers.

"For a fee," Rea said.

"Yes."

"How much? We don't have a lot of money."

"Something you value but can live without. You personally, Mr. Rea."

"Yes, but what?"

"I will decide after the work is done to our mutual satisfaction."

"You want to name any price you like?"

"Yes. It is our usual practice."

"We don't have much. You could destroy us."

"It would be very foolish of us to help you and then destroy you. And I might add that we've never had a complaint."

Ames leaned in and caught Rea's eye. "I've known Hood for years, Mr. Rea. He won't abuse your trust."

Rea and Bethany Scott exchanged a long look. Finally, she nodded yes.

"OK," Rea said. "I guess you're hired."

The group cleared and straightened the room, and Hood led the Llewellyns to guest quarters, where they asked for private time together.

Annie Llewellyn went to a window and gazed out at the swamp. "I'm scared, Pete," she said.

Peter Llewellyn joined her and linked his arm through hers. "Me too, kid."

"And I'm confused."

"About what?"

"The fires. Why a feint? Why are the fires so far a feint? A feint would be a calculated thing. But if you're up to a calculated thing -- a scam or revenge or some such -- a feint doesn't make sense. You wouldn't call attention to yourself before doing your thing. You'd just do it. But if the fires so far are not objectively calculated -- if they're some kind of whacko thing -- then they are not a feint. In Omega's mind, they have some sort of relationship to each other. Some meaning together. But Rea says it's not racial. OK, then, what is it?"

"Oh my, oh my," Peter Llewellyn said. "I wonder if we're still barking up the wrong tree."

Chapter Twenty-Five

Billy Wakefield was a darn lucky kid, and he knew why. He knew a lot of reasons why.

He had a great house, and a lot of neat stuff. His Dad had a great job as a firefighter, which Billy thought was way cool. He liked his school, and he had a lot of friends. He liked church at Jimmy's, although he kept that part pretty much to himself, because his friends might have thought it was kind of dorky. Mom and Dad were great parents, and little Ivy was pretty cute for a baby, and maybe she would grow up to be a cool younger sister. Cool kind of ran in their family, in Billy's opinion.

Billy felt he was a lucky kid for a lot of reasons, but he knew -- sort of in a back part of his mind -- that there was one big reason. He was lucky because he had always felt safe. Billy knew that a lot of people in the world were not safe. And not only the people who were caught in wars and tsunamis and forest fires and that kind of stuff. A lot of people just like Billy and his family were not safe.

You could hear about it on the TV news all the time. People got bad diseases. People lost their jobs. Kids lost one of their parents -- or both of them. Parents lost one of their kids -- or all of them. Families came apart (maybe Sammy Winthrop's, for example.)

It seemed to Billy that you just never knew when something might blow into your life and make a big mess of it. And that was the other side of that feeling in the back of Billy's mind. The other side of feeling like you had safety was knowing that it could be taken away from you. So, when the church-burning thing started to disturb the rhythms of Billy's life, he got worried.

It wasn't exactly a specific thing that he could put his finger on. More of a kind of change in the air. In the way things worked. For starters, there had been some tense feeling at home. There had never been tense feeling at home before. Not this way. Mom was super worried, for starters. And yes, Mom had always been kind of a worrywart about Dad's safety, but this was bigger, and different.

And Dad had been kind of tired, and on edge. He was still nice. He didn't yell or anything. But you could see in his face that he was sort of carrying an extra load. There was a lot of tension at work, Dad said, because the firefighters really wanted to see the Omega guy get caught. The firefighters didn't like seeing things get burned down on their watch. Dad himself said that very thing a lot. *I don't' like this on my watch.* Billy was confused about what the fires had to do with wristwatches until Dad explained that it was a way of talking about being officially on guard duty.

There had been a lot of tension for the firefighters, and they got tired, too, because the commanders had them putting in extra hours to search for what the Omega guy might have set up to start more fires. The searching got really heavy, Dad said, when the commanders were told that the first fires probably weren't just aimed at black people, so that meant there were a lot more places to search and a lot more things to think about. Dad said the commanders were worried that the first fires were a feint. Billy was confused about what bad fires had to do with passing out, until Dad explained that it was spelled a different way and meant that somebody faked doing one thing to distract attention from what they really meant to do.

And then Uncle Toby made things even worse. He didn't mean to, of course. He meant to help. Like when he suggested that the fire stations could be collection points for stuff to help the church people.

Uncle Toby said everyone needed to be thinking about what he called a worst-case scenario. And preparing for it. Uncle Toby said -- to the bosses at the fire department, among other people -- that the worst-case scenario was that Omega was a firefighter. In that case, he would be really good at setting something up and hiding it, and he could have hidden it somewhere a long time ago and just be waiting to set it off. Also, he could have hidden it just about anywhere, because firefighters were all over town all the time with inspections and presentations and stuff.

Dad actually got a little peeved at Uncle Toby over it, because having one of their own suggest that Omega could be a firefighter made the commanders even more worried, which meant they put even more pressure on to find and stop whatever Omega had planned, and Dad said they were already doing everything they could be expected to do. Dad said it was another case of Uncle Toby trying to prove himself, and since they were already doing all they could be expected to do, it was an unnecessary complication. Dad wished that just this once, Uncle Toby had left well enough alone.

But Billy happened to know that Uncle Toby wasn't just trying to prove himself. He was really worried. He had talked about it when Billy was over at his house and they were playing trains (which Billy was beginning to lose a little interest in, because Aunt Inez's yelling at Uncle Toby had gotten to be pretty much a full-time thing, just like Billy wasn't really there, and Billy thought it was really unpleasant and not a nice way for her to behave at all).

Uncle Toby said that Omega was a real problem for the community because he had to be a very strong and resourceful man to do what he had done, keeping a whole town on edge and all that. (Billy had to ask Dad what resourceful meant. He didn't tell him why.) And Uncle Toby said Omega had to be smart, too, to set up those remote control and motion-activated switches to start the fires, because that kind of thing was pretty darned complicated. Billy figured Uncle Toby knew what he was talking about there, since he had all that automatic stuff set up around the train set to open bridges and crossing gates and turn on lights and switch trains from track to track and all kinds of stuff.

So, Uncle Toby was worried that Omega was a way serious problem. And Mom was worried, and Dad was worried, and pretty much the whole town was worried, and Billy didn't feel as safe as he had before, and he didn't like that one bit. He figured maybe he should talk to Father Pete about it.

Chapter Twenty-Six

Lew Perry drove his black Silverado south and east into gathering twilight. In the passenger seat, Ames Colville watched the sandy flats of eastern North Carolina slide by.

"Nice people, your friends," Lew said.

"Yes. The best. Their family has lived around here for a long time. Yeoman stock."

"You're different when you're with them."

"Maybe. I'm more comfortable with those folks than with most. They're genuine. No pose, no pretense, no keeping up with the Joneses. I guess maybe there's a part of me that doesn't like too much of what passes for civilization."

"Well, I have to say that Mrs. Godwin's biscuits were pretty darned civilized. Never had anything like them."

Ames chuckled. "That's the only part of life where she allows herself to be prideful. I guess she's justified."

"And how."

Ames fished a cellphone from his pocket. "Guess we'd better update Hood. I'll put him on speaker."

Hood answered on the second ring. "Hello."

"Ames here. We have the information."

"And?"

"The checks are made to Doar, but they go to an office address in Raleigh."

"Three hours from his office in Charlotte. He's not manning the Raleigh place personally. Not by himself anyway. Does the office address have a name associated with it? A person? An organization?"

"Not for mailing purposes. Just a street address and office number."

"Text it to me when we're done. I'll ask Larkin to check it out."

"Will do. Anything new at your end?"

"Afraid so. There's been another fire and another message."

"Bad?"

"Bad enough. Another dumpster fire. This one behind Lincoln Middle School. But the note is ominous."

"How so?"

"He rambles about this fire being the last one without deaths. He teases about how many deaths there will be. He intimates that there will be a lot. And he has shortened the time frame. He says he's tired of the game. Instead of the next fire being on or after November 8, he now says the day will simply be November 8. Any time in the 24 hours beginning at midnight."

"Damn. Has Aimee turned up any new leads?"

"Maybe. She's found that arson is not common in this area. But one case is interesting.

Wilmington, 15 years ago. A house fire killed a man and his wife. Faculty members at UNC Wilmington. They had a teenage son who was never found. There was no third body in the fire, no trace of the boy anywhere afterward. He simply disappeared.   The story that emerged about the family afterward was pretty grim. The parents wanted the boy to be a student superstar. They pushed him relentlessly about performance in school. Punished him if he fell short of perfection in any subject. Ridiculed him in public for any shortcoming. Neighbors suspected the boy of acting out in revenge. Pets disappeared or were killed. Property vandalized. Nothing was ever proved, however."

"And the fire was arson?" Ames said.

"Yes. The authorities theorized that the boy burned his own home down and then ran away. And there's one more thing. About the parents' academic fields."

"Yes?"

"The father was an expert on the classics. The mother taught English literature."

"Claudius and Gulliver," Ames said.

"Precisely. It appears that Omega quite likely is the angry boy become angry man."

"None of which is particularly helpful in figuring out who he is today or what he may do on November 8."

"Regrettably, no."

"Well, we are headed back to Yaupon Bay. We'll check in there with the citizen surveillance and official Omega search efforts, and with Gloster's team of volunteer watchers. What is next for you?"

"I checked on Clyde Hunter. He has indeed gone to ground. He's nowhere to be found. Aimee and I worked on the lists of donor intermediaries and identified a couple of especially heavy givers. I'm headed to Charlotte tomorrow. Although he doesn't know it, I have a date with a dentist."

"Good hunting."

"Thanks."

Ames ended the call and lowered his passenger window slightly to let in the evening air.

"Mind?" he said. "I love anticipating the time when you get close enough to smell the salt water."

"Not at all," Lew said.

"How are you doing on the real estate story?"

"Well, I'm sort of stymied for now. The lawyers' dog and pony show in Charlotte didn't really get me anywhere useful. And to tell the truth, I'm struggling about what is the right thing to do."

"Meaning?"

"It's the dilemma of not really having the option of doing nothing. Just minding my own business and walking away. If I write a story and complicate the development, I'm harming some of the people who would benefit from the project. But If I just give up and write nothing, I'm harming the landowners who won't get a competitive price for their land. I don't like having that kind of power. Or, to be more precise, I don't like not having the option of laying it down."

"Comes with the profession, Lew. If you're in a position to put words into print, you're automatically more powerful than your neighbors. And there is an essential unfairness in it. They didn't elect you. They can't vote against you. But you can affect their lives for better or for worse just because you choose to. If you keep on with a life as a journalist, you'll have to find a way to live with that, but never be comfortable with it. If you get comfortable with it, you'll get reckless."

Lew lifted one hand from the steering wheel and stroked the back of his neck.

"Ames?" he said.

"Yes?"

"I have to leave. I have to leave The Sand Dollar and Yaupon Bay."

"Tell me why."

"Because that's how I will finish learning who I am as a man. You've talked to me about that. So has my Dad. I've thought about it a lot. I don't have all the answers yet, by a long shot. But I do know a few things. Finding out who I am is not just about -- well, about finding out. Some of it also is about deciding.

"If I go for the brass ring, as you call it, and I fail, then I'll have to make some decision about who I am in life. If I get the brass ring but it isn't what I expected, then the same thing. Some decisions about who I am in life. If I get the brass ring and I like it, then I'll have to make some decisions about how to live that life. I like living in Yaupon Bay, and I love working with you at The Sand Dollar. But I just fell into it. I didn't decide on this life. I have to go to the effort of thinking about decisions. I have to try to learn more about myself. And I can only do that if I leave."

He laid his free hand on Ames' shoulder.

"I owe you a lot. I hope you're not disappointed in me."

Ames smiled in the darkness. "Not a bit disappointed. I care about you. I think you know that. I think you've made the right decision for the right reasons. Godspeed, son. And you'll always have access to your friends here. I'm not the only one who cares about you."

They drove on in silence. Ames was beginning to doze when Lew abruptly pulled onto the shoulder, braked to a stop and exclaimed, "Holy shit!"

"What? What's wrong?" Ames said.

"Access. I didn't notice it at the time. The access was wrong."

"What are you talking about?"

"The dog and pony show those lawyers gave me in Charlotte. The architect's rendering of the development. The vehicular access was on the wrong side."

"How so?"

"The development in Yaupon Bay will be between The Highway and The Barren. There is no leeway for how it could be arranged. Vehicular access would have to come from The Highway side. From the east. But the access on the drawings they showed me was from the west. For people to drive into the Yaupon Bay development from the west side, they'd have to be coming out of the swamp."

"Which suggests that the lawyers who met with you aren't familiar with the particulars of the Yaupon Bay project."

"Right."

"And it suggests that the lawyer -- or lawyers -- actually handling the project doesn't want to meet you."

"And the question is, why not? And, for that matter, why show me a fake rendering? Why not show me something genuine? I'd already agreed to confidentiality."

"I can make a couple of guesses."

"And they are …?"

"They didn't want you to meet the real project lawyer because something about him or them would tell you something they don't want you to know. And they didn't show you a real rendering because there isn't one."

"So, what are they hiding?"

"And who?"

Chapter Twenty-Seven

Elwood P. Hollister, D.D.S., hated his first name. He always had. From boyhood he had insisted on being known as E.P. Even his disappointed mother -- who had dubbed him Elwood -- eventually gave in. She called him E.P. His father called him E.P. His friends called him E.P. To the whole world, he was E.P -- except to a certain traitorous part of himself. Now and then, without warning, his full first name would flash in his mind's eye: *Elwood.* He was Elwood, now and forever, world without end, amen, and he hated it.

But he had to admit that the name thing was about the only blemish on a life that was, all things considered, pretty damn rosy. His dental practice was thriving. His home was a showplace. His Cadillac was a dandy. His wife was good to him. He was popular at the club, where he was able to get in enough golf to establish a pretty decent handicap.

And his only son -- the apple of his eye -- had decided to follow in his footsteps and enter dental school. In the pride department, E.P. Hollister thought, that was pretty much a button-popper. The boy admired him. The boy wanted to be like dad. One of E.P.'s fondest memories was the night Brad (not Elwood junior by a long damn shot) had told him. They had gone over to the club to celebrate with a couple of drinks. After a couple, and a couple more, they had set about formally toasting the three essential tenets of family dentistry: *Drill, fill and bill.* They toasted several times -- so emphatically that they were beginning to get fishy looks from the bartender, and E.P. decided that discretion called for withdrawal to home. He didn't want to damage his image at the club, after all.

Yes, life had been good to Elwood P. Hollister, D.D.S. Life and the free enterprise system, which in his opinion was under attack by liberal do-gooders and fatheaded politicians who taxed the hell out of successful men to fund handouts to the whiners and slackers who kept voting them into office. It was a shame, as all his friends at the club heartily agreed. He enjoyed his post-work ritual of joining them for a drink and an assessment of the piss-poor state of public affairs.

He was therefore a trifle annoyed as he went to leave work and found in his waiting room an elegant black man whose smile was oddly intimidating. He was doubly annoyed to note that his receptionist had skipped early and left him alone with this interruption of his routine.

"I'm sorry sir," he said. "Our office is closed for the day. If you have an emergency, I can refer you to a clinic."

"I'm not here for dental work," the man said, rising and offering a business card.

The card said, "Marcus Lenta, Consultant."

"Well, then, what can I help you with?" Hollister said, hoping that edge on his voice was evident.

"Politics," the man said, maintaining that smile.

"Now look, if you're after contributions, I give directly."

"I know," the man said.

"What?"

"Your name is in the campaign finance reports. They are public record."

"Then what do you want?"

"Sit down, Dr. Hollister, and let's talk."

The smile persuaded Hollister that sitting down for a talk was probably a good idea.

"All right, how can I help you?" he said, hoping that the disappearance of an edge from his voice was not evident.

"I want information on your political contributions. For example, how are you told who you should give to?"

"I give as I please. It's my money."

"No, it's not. Not all of it, anyway."

"I beg your pardon?"

"You receive checks from a third party. A fund of some sort. Perhaps the checks are signed by a man named Daniel Doar."

"It's still my business. It's a free country."

"Some of what you are doing is not properly your own private business."

"Who are you, anyway?"

"One of your fellow citizens. A fellow citizen whose personal welfare and civil rights are affected by your behavior. You are receiving money from people with extreme right-wing views. You are giving it to politicians of their choosing."

"I give to politicians whose positions are on the public record."

"You give to politicians who are lying by omission. The people who send you money are white supremacists, Dr. Hollister. The politicians you support are disguising their real views to consolidate power they intend to use for purposes undeclared. As a practical matter, Dr. Hollister, you are a short step from being a practicing neo-Nazi."

"I emphatically deny this. There is no evidence of it. There can't be, because it isn't true."

"The people you're in bed with keep records. There is a ledger. Your name is in it, and your address, and records of financial transactions."

"Anybody could create a ledger. That doesn't mean what's in it is true."

"What's in that ledger doesn't have to be true, Dr. Hollister. It only has to be interesting to your friends, family, peers and patients. Gossip can be such an ugly and hurtful thing. In any case, I'm quite confident that the ledger is accurate. It reflects money passing in and out of a certain fund. A fund means bank accounts, and bank accounts mean records. Incontrovertible records."

In his mind's eye, Elwood P. Hollister's first name appeared. It was chiseled from stone. The stone was conspicuously cracked. The cracks, he knew, represented damage to his image at the club. In the community. His after-work drinking companions talked a good game, but he knew that in their hearts they were dilettantes. Poseurs. Men who would be daunted by any prospect of action with real consequences. Men who would turn their backs on him if his name became controversial. And they were not the only ones who would turn away.

"You are blackmailing me," Hollister said.

"You are a drone, Dr. Hollister. Only a drone. I have no interest in harming you or, quite frankly, in any prolonged transaction with you. I only want information. If you give it, I will leave. I will conceal your betrayal from the people in control. They are the ones I want to reach."

"What do you want? Specifically, what do you want?"

"You've handled a good deal of money for these people."

"Yes."

"You would have files. Records."

"Yes. Here in my office safe."

"I want to see copies of the instructions you receive on giving to candidates. And I want to see copies of the checks you're sent. I want to see all of it, from the beginning."

The man was quite thorough, and quite demanding. They were at it for a long time. Hollister missed his after-work drink session at the club. And throughout the whole thing, the man's unsettling smile never wavered. In the months afterward, Hollister would now and then see it in his dreams.

Chapter Twenty-Eight

"Do you get those pickets every Sunday?" Larkin asked.

"No," Peter Llewellyn said. "They have a list of churches they consider to be too gay- friendly. They go from one to another. We get them about once every six weeks."

"Ugly bunch," Aimee said.

"Well, their message certainly is. But they're really not terribly aggressive or disruptive. The core group is only two or three people. They recruit others to come along as they can. The recruits come a time or two and then get bored with it. They move on and other recruits show up. They wave their *God Hates Fags* signs and do their chants about eternal damnation, and then I go out and meet with them and ask if they would please be quiet while we are conducting our worship service. They lay hands on me and pray for my soul, and by the time we come out after the service they've gone."

They were gathered in the parish hall, sipping and munching leftovers from the church coffee hour. Billy Wakefield eyed Hood and company with conspicuous curiosity until his Mom whispered something in his ear. The others heard only the word *polite.*

"And that's about it for excitement," Llewellyn said. "No obvious moves by the Doar people."

"No obvious ones," Hood said. "But it's unlikely they let the opportunity pass by completely. They could have checked the lay of the land. How heavily the service is attended; how long it lasts; what the patterns of movement are; where all the entrances and exits are located; that sort of thing. It could have been any visitor."

"We did have a few," Llewellyn said. "But we always do. Only one spoke to me afterward. The rest slipped away, but that's common too."

He turned to Billy Wakefield.

"Billy, is it alright if we have our talk here, in front of this lady and these gentlemen? They are helping me with some problems, and they need to stay nearby."

Sarah Jane Wakefield caught her son's eye and mouthed the same word: *Polite.*

"Yes sir," Billy said.

"Tell me what's on your mind."

"Well, first I need your help with a word. It means that something could happen but it isn't or maybe it's happening but it's not happening to you where you are. So, there is a word that says what you're doing when you talk about stuff like that."

"I think you mean *abstract,*" Peter Llewellyn said. "When you talk about things like that, you're talking about them in the abstract."

"Yes," Billy said. "That's it. Well before, when we were talking about why God lets bad things happen?"

"Yes?"

"For me, we were kind of talking about that in the abstract."

"But now we're not."

"No," Billy said. "We're not. The bad things that are going on with the fires? Now, they have started to hurt my Mom and Dad a lot worse and a lot more personally. And I don't like it. I don't like it that they are being hurt, and I don't like it that I can't do anything about it. That I can't help them."

"So, what you're saying is that you are angry."

"Yes."

"You are angry at God."

Billy looked down at the floor, over at his parents, back at Peter Llewellyn.

"Is it alright to say that?"

"Yes, it is."

"It's OK to be angry at God?"

"Yes, it's OK."

"I don't like being angry at God, Father Pete. Can't you help me?"

"Well, Billy, do you remember the last time we talked, and I said that sometimes the answers I gave you would seem to make a lot of sense and sometimes they would seem to make no sense at all? But that they were things it was good to think about anyway?"

"Yes."

"I'm afraid that's still where we are, Billy. I can't make your parents' hurt or yours go away. You're going to think I haven't helped you much, but I want to give you another thing to think about. It's this: When you look at life, it's a good thing to remember to look at all of it. Not just the ugly parts. I call it taking a whole look. And if you take a whole look today, Billy, you could see that along with the hurt, your parents have a great and wonderful blessing."

"What is it?"

"You, Billy. A son who loves them so much he dares to be angry at God."

Billy Wakefield looked down at the floor, back up at Peter Llewellyn.

"Father Pete, it's like you said. That doesn't feel like it helps much."

"Well, it helps at least a little. It helps your parents. Look at them."

Billy looked and saw that Mom had tears running down her cheeks but was smiling at the same time, and Dad was kind of huffing and puffing like he was having trouble catching his breath.

"I'm really going to have to think hard about that one, Father Pete. But thank you for trying to help me. Can I go to the library for a while? I think better there."

"Sure," Peter Llewellyn said.

Billy's parents nodded *yes.* He kissed each of them on the cheek and hurried out.

"Quite a lad," Hood said.

"Yes," Bill Wakefield croaked. "He is."

"Fewer than twelve hours until the eighth," Hood said. "Are you on duty tonight?"

`   "On call," Bill Wakefield said. "All of us who aren't working a shift are on call or helping with the search."

"How is that working?" Annie Llewellyn asked.

"The fire department is taking the lead, because we have the expertise. The police and the citizen surveillance volunteers are also pitching in. We are looking for any clue that might signal what Omega's next target is. Ideally, he has set up his ignition system in advance and we'll find it before he can set it off. At the same time, we're checking on response capacities in case he isn't stopped. The search is organized around worst-case casualty scenarios. Nighttime targets would be apartment projects, bars, clubs, that sort of thing. Daytime targets would be schools, shopping malls and such. Hospitals and nursing homes would be round-the-clock targets."

"And nothing has been found?" Annie Llewellyn said.

"Not so far. There is so much territory to cover."

"I still think something is being missed. Something about the first set of fires."

"What do you mean?"

"That man Rea said the first fires weren't really racially motivated. So we assumed that the racial aspect was some kind of feint. Something else was going on. Something calculated. Insurance fraud. Revenge arson. Something of that sort. But in a context of calculation, a feint doesn't make sense. If you're going to commit arson for hire, for example, you don't put the whole town on alert for weeks beforehand, you just do it."

"Go on," Bill Wakefield said.

"So, if the first fires weren't a feint," Annie Llewellyn said, "they were something else. They are tied together somehow in the mind of the arsonist. If the tie isn't race hatred, then what is it? That's what we're missing."

"Interesting," Bill Wakefield said. "Interesting."

Billy appeared in the parish hall door with a white envelope in hand.

"Father Pete? A man came to the library. He asked me to give this to you."

Hood stiffened in his chair.

"What kind of man?" he said. "What did he look like? What did he say?"

"He looked average. He was about my Dad's age, I guess. He didn't really say anything except to give the envelope to Father Pete. He was very polite."

Larkin bolted for the door. Peter Llewellyn opened the envelope and read aloud.

"If you will check the left-hand front pocket of your trousers, you will find a 1987 penny. A small notch has been filed in the edge of the coin, just above Lincoln's head. I slipped it into your pocket when we clustered around you to pray for your soul.

"I could have killed you on the spot and escaped in the confusion. The protesters would have been blamed for a while. Religious zealots have such a bad image. But probably you have correctly surmised that while your elderly friend remains at large we wouldn't do such a thing.

"Just consider this a kind of advice. An alert. We are everywhere. You can't avoid or escape us. Sooner or later, we will find you in a vulnerable position, and we will take you away for some persuasion about finding your friend. Of course, if we find him first, your life will become worthless. You don't know what you have offered to uncover. You never will.

"And by the way, your bodyguards are conspicuous. The big man with the penetrating eyes. The smaller one with the athletic body language. The young woman with the remarkably intelligent face. We've marked them now. Their value to you is compromised.

"Food for thought."

"One of the protesters' recruits," Peter Llewellyn said. He fished in his pocket and held up the coin.

"They want to frighten you," Hood said. "Frightened people make bad decisions."

Larkin rejoined the group.

"No one," he said. "Not in the building and not outside."

"He wouldn't linger," Hood said.

"Think it was Jesse Hoyt?"

"It certainly wasn't the work of one of Doar's has-beens. We should alert Ames that matters seem to be escalating. Father Llewellyn, does this building have an alarm system?"

"Yes. Why do you ask?"

"Our unavoidably urgent issue is Omega. We have a bout of waiting to do, until developments begin after midnight. The man who left the letter was most certainly a professional. He was in the building, and will have checked for an alarm system. He wouldn't risk setting it off, and he wouldn't risk disabling it, because either event would alert the police. He couldn't be sure of their reaction time. He couldn't count on having time enough to deal with us and take you."

"You mean we might as well do our waiting here."

"Yes."

"Makes sense. There are food and drink in the kitchen. We have cots if anyone wants to stretch out."

"I think Billy and I will go home," Sarah Jane Wakefield said. She looked at her husband. "Bill?"

"I think I will stay here," he said. "That way, if I get a call, I won't disturb you and Billy."

"Very well," Hood said. "Let's get on with it." He picked up Peter Llewellyn's note. "What an interesting turn of phrase," he said.

"What do you mean?" Llewellyn said.

"We are everywhere."

Chapter Twenty-Nine

Bill Wakefield paced the perimeter of the room, pausing occasionally to gaze at a wall-mounted clock whose minute hand was creeping past 11:30. Peter and Annie Llewellyn played chess on a card table. Hood, Aimee and Larkin sipped coffee on a recycled pew that sat against a wall beneath a bank of windows.

Any hitches in the Fayetteville operation?" Hood asked.

"No," Larkin said. "It went smoothly."

"How did you do it?" Peter Llewellyn asked, waiting for Annie's move.

"Larkin used one of our fake registrations to tie the truck to an empty warehouse here in Yaupon Bay," Hood said. "We want to draw their attention here. He made sure the surveillance cameras at the storage place got a good look at the truck. We put our own cameras on the warehouse to see if anyone pays it unusual attention. Gloster's people will help with the watching, too."

"What about the truck?" Llewellyn said.

"It's ours," Hood said. "We use it in our undertakings from time to time. We'll hold onto the arms and explosives for now. When the theft has served its purposes, we may have an opportunity to help the authorities tie them back to Doar and Jesse Hoyt. If not, we'll arrange for the authorities to find them and dispose of them."

"And the message to Doar?"

"As I suggested," Hood said. "Larkin broke into Doar's Charlotte office and painted it on the wall. *I stole your toys from Fayetteville. John Smith.*"

"Why do you want to draw their attention to Yaupon Bay?"

"It simplifies our surveillance, and it heightens the possibility that they'll see Ames'
picture in The Sand Dollar. "

"How did Lew handle that?"

"Deftly. Ames is often mentioned in their letters to the editor. Lew put a small photo in one of them. It's there to be seen, if anyone looks, but not so blatant as to be obvious bait. The Doar people will nonetheless consider the possibility that it is bait, but it tells them the big thing they want to know: Who John Smith really is. They'll nibble. Cautiously, but they'll nibble. We've rigged the newspaper office and Ames' apartment with interior lights that go on and off in a random pattern, as if the quarters were occupied. We've hidden more cameras outside, and once again the Gloster people will help with the watching."

"And if you can identify someone snooping at the warehouse or The Sand Dollar? What happens then?"

"You don't want to know too much about that," Hood said.

On the chessboard, Annie Llewellyn made her move.

"Check," she said.

Peter Llewellyn eyed the board for a long moment.

"Damn! How did you do that?"

Annie Llewellyn rose and headed for the kitchen.

"I'm taking a break. You'll be a while figuring out how to get out of that one."

Peter Llewellyn pushed back from the table and rubbed his eyes.

"Can you tell us what you learned from the dentist in Charlotte?" he said.

"We knew from Ames' friends that the original contributions are made to Doar but sent to an office in Raleigh. The check to the dentist was signed by Doar but drawn on an account in the name of an organization that calls itself 'Restore Our State.' The letters directing the dentist's contributions were on the organization's letterhead. They were also signed by Doar."

"Doar is in Charlotte; the dentist is in Charlotte; but the transaction is handled through an office three hours away. Sounds oddly complicated."

"Indeed. We've agreed that Larkin will break into the Raleigh office to see what more we can learn."

Across the room, Bill Wakefield kicked a metal trash can and shouted "Damn!"

All eyes went to him.

"Annie was right. There is something connecting the fires Omega has set so far. Annie was right, dammit! If it isn't racial, and it isn't some sort of scam or scheme, then the obvious thing that's left is pyromania. We've got ourselves a firebug."

"That's the connection? "Peter Llewellyn said. "That's what the fires have in common? A pyromaniac? I don't see how that helps solve it. We already knew what Aimee found about the kid in Wilmington years ago. And we already speculated that he might be Omega. We assumed -- or at last I did -- that the fire that killed his parents was simple revenge. But maybe the revenge motive was just a trigger, and pyromania was the underlying thing with him. So, if we define these fires here in Yaupon Bay as pyromania, we haven't really learned much new."

"That's not what I'm driving at," Bill Wakefield said. "Pyromaniacs notoriously like to watch the fires they've set. The thing connecting the fires so far is that they were all in the coverage area of one fire station. Mine. My station was called to all the fires. Omega can count on watching the fires he's set without being an obvious voyeur because … "

"He's a firefighter," Hood said. "Your friend said as much. He told the fire department command to be alert to the possibility that Omega is a firefighter."

"Toby Butler. Yes. He said it could be."

Bill Wakefield's cell phone rang. He fished it out of his pocket and checked the display.

"My wife," He said. "Have to take this."

As he listened, Bill Wakefield's face went slack, then white.

"He said what? Oh, my God."

He ended the call and turned to the group.

"Billy wouldn't go to sleep after they got home. He was obsessed with trying to help. With not feeling useless. My wife has been trying to calm him all evening, but he insisted on talking about it. Just now, finally, he said that we should let his Uncle Toby lead the search for whatever Omega has set up. Uncle Toby is Toby Butler. He said Toby would know how to spot Omega's setup because he would know exactly what it would look like. It would be like the picture of the ignition device that Bob Greenlee has on his desk. Billy said Toby has several of the exact same things set up to control his train sets."

"But the fire department has been leading the searches," Peter Llewellyn said. "They would know what kind of thing to look for. They've found nothing."

Hood bolted up from his chair.

"Because there's nothing to find," he said. "By suggesting that Omega could be a firefighter, Toby Butler misdirected attention and spread search resources all over Yaupon Bay."

"What exactly do you mean? He misdirected attention?"

"He directed it away from himself, by being the person who made the suggestion. And he directed it away from the place he's going to torch tonight. One of the few places that hasn't been exhaustively searched, because the searchers were away from it, focusing elsewhere."

"Oh, my God," Bill Wakefield said. "The fire station. He's going to torch our fire station."

"Yes. We have to get there. Father Llewellyn, Mrs. Llewellyn, you will have to come with us. We can't afford to leave you alone. And as a matter of fact, you can help. On our way, Father Llewellyn, you can call the police."

"And tell them what?" Peter Llewellyn said. "That I've figured out what a small army of experts couldn't?"

"Lie to them. Tell them you're Omega, and you're going to torch the fire station, and they can't stop you. They won't be able to ignore that. And as soon as you've alerted the police, call Toby Butler's wife. Tell her to rush to the fire station and bring his hairbrush."

Chapter Thirty

Omega whistled while he worked. He whistled because he was feeling pretty damn good about himself. The whole town was looking for him. The feds, too. But they hadn't been able to find him. They hadn't figured him out, because he was cautious, and pretty damn smart.

Yes, cautious, he thought, as he padlocked the chain through the handles of the double door to the living quarters of the firehouse. Time for a little payback. Or a lot. He was pretty generally irked by firehouse life among men who considered him a second-class member of the team. Even when he did things on calls that they didn't have the balls to do, they looked down on him. He could tell. They weren't mean or even unkind. But they looked down. It irked him.

The chain might not really be necessary, he knew. He had pretty carefully drugged their food and drinks. But who knew how someone might react if they woke a little when the flames reached them, and they had even a few seconds to get juiced up by panic? The chain might not be necessary, but it was the cautious thing to do.

And yes, he was pretty damn smart to suggest that the guy they were all looking for might be a firefighter. The notion would have occurred to someone sooner or later. But the guy they were looking for wouldn't rat on himself, now would he? It was so easy to out-think the Lilliputians.

He was smart, too, when he arranged to be scheduled to work the shift. The fire was going to be pretty damn hot. At some point the diesel in the trucks would go up, too. They would be a long time sorting through what little remained of the bodies. By the time they figured out he wasn't among them, he would be long gone. He would have to create a new identity, yes. And that was a pain in the neck, he knew, from doing it before. But he could do it again.

He was going to cause a lot of suffering. He knew that, too, and a part of him regretted it. But strong men did what was necessary. Inez had made it necessary. You could say that, if you looked at it a certain way. She never should have started yelling at him. She never should have called him a *kid.* Inez had no idea what being a kid was like for him.

The very word made it come roaring back at him. *Kid.* It was a synonym for everything the strong man must deny. Must reject. Must belie. Mom and Dad hounding and belittling a child. Mater and Pater, as they called themselves when they were full-on batshit crazy, prancing around him in circles screaming and sneering. Making an example of him to himself, whatever the hell that meant. Scourging him they said, to make strength emerge.

Well, strength had emerged, alright, and boy were they surprised. At least he supposed they were surprised, if they woke from their drugged sleep to find their bedroom door locked, their window nailed shut and their home rapidly becoming an inferno. He read some of the newspaper stories afterward, while he was hiding. Before he started running. They said the fire was arson. *Check.* They speculated he had done it. *Well, who else?* They called Mater and Pater respected academics. *Nobody asked me.* They called it monstrous.

Now, that was a hurtful word. He thought about it for a long time. And he finally decided that he was not monstrous. No, not the real himself. He decided that the Omega part of him had done it. And if it was a pretty darned serious thing to do, yes it was, it was necessary. He decided that only the Omega part of him would do that kind of necessary thing, and that the real himself would live his new daily life and be among regular people and get on with his future. He decided that the Omega part of him might never have to emerge again. Surely nothing like the first Omega thing would ever be necessary again.

So, he locked the Omega part away, and for years the real himself was -- well, himself. And then Inez started in with the yelling and the belittling. With the *kid* thing. She pried the lock off the door, and out came Omega, the strong man who would do what was necessary, who would show her, -- who would show the world -- that what she said was a damn lie. She was just one more Lilliputian. He was the strong man.

She deserved to be punished for it. Any fair-minded person would say so. He had considered torching the house -- with her inside, of course -- at the same time he torched the station. It would be easy to do with the devices he had built.

But then he decided that she should instead live for the rest of her life with the identity she would eventually acquire: She would be the woman who lived for years with a monster and was so blind and stupid that she never saw it. They would call him a monster again. He knew that. But he was the strong man. He could withstand whatever came, if it was part of doing what was necessary. Inez was the Lilliputian who would live with lifelong humiliation.

Toby Butler was double-checking his setup when blue lights began flashing against the walls of the truck bay and he saw police cruisers pulling up to circle the fire station. It occurred to him that something had gone wrong. That they meant to stop him. What else could they he about, these Lilliputians? Far-fetched as the very notion was, it occurred to him that something in his plan had gone wrong.

Well, time later to figure out the *yes* or the *no* of that. For whatever reason, they were here, and they were leaving their cars and coming toward him, and he couldn't let that go on.
He stepped to an open bay door and held the ignition device over his head.

"Stop where you are, or I'll blow this station up right now."

They stopped in their tracks. Radios crackled and spoke. Cops in front of him talking to cops who'd circled around behind. One cop stepped forward. A commander or something by the look of him. Stars and bars and stuff all over his uniform.

"Put the device down, please, Mr. Butler. This is not a good thing to do. Please let's talk this over. Put the device down."

But of course, if he put it down, they would swarm him and his plan would never be completed, and he couldn't have that. But if he set it off, he would die right along with the others, which had never been part of his plan, and he couldn't have that. So, it occurred to him that he had a dilemma. But he couldn't have that, either. Strong men didn't have dilemmas. They had plans of action.

He would think of one. He knew he would. He just needed a little time.

"Put the device down, Mr. Butler."

"Never," he answered in the voice of a strong man.

He liked that voice. It occurred to him that maybe the real himself should have used it a little more often.

"Never," he shouted again.

And then the line of cops parted and a clergyman stepped forward. And stepping right with him was a big black fellow who walked like he was a strong man himself, or maybe a king or a prince or something. And this was pretty damn confusing, because they just kept on walking right up to him, which they should have been afraid to do, because they were Lilliputians and he had the device in his hand and needed only to twitch his thumb. Then in the gap behind them he saw Inez, of all people, which was pretty damn confusing all by itself, and she was holding -- *a hairbrush?*

"Please, Mr. Butler," the clergyman called out. "Don't do this to your friends. To your family. Put the device down."

"Never," Toby Butler roared again.

And again, it sounded good. At least he had that part right.

The clergyman slowed and stopped, but the big man kept right on coming. Not saying a word, just coming and coming. And when he was close enough for them to have man-to-man eye contact, he held up his right hand with his thumb and forefinger pinched together like he was holding onto something really fine or tiny.

And then TobyOmegaButlerKid heard a sound that reminded him of wind in faraway treetops. The others heard it, too. He could see them looking up and around.

And the big man kept right on coming and coming. Not saying a word, just coming and coming. And TobyOmegaButlerKid began having notions and seeing images and hearing sounds. The first notion he had was that the device in his hand was a despicable, ugly thing, and he didn't want to hold it or even have it near him. He put it down and kicked it away.

The images were awful beyond his wildest imagination, and the sounds offered to split his skull. The others couldn't see or hear those, he knew, because they were standing quietly by as if it were only a mild November evening and the sight and sounds of hell were not roaring in their presence.

His last conscious awareness for several days was this: He was hugging the ankles of the big man and screaming and weeping and begging for the images and the sounds to stop and the feet of others were circling up around him and then the torture stopped and they were lifting up by his arms and he faded into merciful blackness.

Chapter Thirty-One

"How's the boy?" Hood said.

"Confused; hurt; probably a little frightened," Peter Llewellyn said. "He thought of Butler as a family member."

"You'll help him, I'm sure."

"I'll try, if he will let me. He feels I let him down. No, actually, that's too antiseptic a way to put it. He feels I peddled bullshit to him."

Annie Llewellyn put a hand on his forearm. He covered it with one of his.

"We'll see what time brings," Peter Llewellyn said. "Let's get to work."

They were seated again in a circle of easy chairs. The sound system was silent. November morning sunlight slanted into the room, throwing long shadows.

Larkin led the conversation.

"Here is what we know from Hood's visit to the dentist and my look inside the Raleigh office. I'm going to include a bit of conjecture, but I think we can reasonably do that. We began, of course, with Daniel Doar. Well, Doar is a front. He does not make decisions. He doesn't even actually handle the money that flows in his name.

"The Raleigh office is a mail drop and a filing center. It contains no computers, no phones, no working equipment of any kind. One set of files is devoted to holding documents with Doar's signature on them. Deposit slips; checks; letterhead. All blank except for Doar's signature at the bottom. All of them match the checks and letters received by the dentist. They purport to be from an organization called Restore Our State.

"The initial contributions are made out to Doar but mailed to the Raleigh office. The blank deposit slips are used by someone else to put the money in the organization account. The same someone else -- or others, for all we know -- uses the checks and the stationery to send money and letters to the intermediaries over Doar's signature."

"But what about the ledger?" Lew Perry said. "The one you found in his office. It showed him keeping track of funds coming and going."

"He wasn't creating the ledger. He was receiving it. To help him maintain the appearance of his front. Whoever controlled the money sent him the information. If any of his donors ever asked questions, he could give credible answers."

"Hunter did imply there was someone above Doar," Peter Llewellyn said. "Someone who could call the shots. So, the Raleigh office is a link. We could watch it. Put surveillance on it."

"I see a problem there," Hood said. "The financial activity is tied to political cycles. This year's big election season is over. There's not another until next year. It could be weeks or even months before the Raleigh office sees any activity."

"And waiting is not a good idea," Larkin said. "Only one set of files pertained to Doar. There were 24 other sets. There are 24 other Doars, scattered from one end of the state to another.   That would have each of them covering about four counties. Their money is handled through 25 separate bank accounts. This white supremacist political movement is carefully organized state-wide."

Peter Llewellyn whistled. "So what do we do? How do we penetrate that?"

"Well," Hood said, "our Ames-as-John-Smith ploy has already been burned. We might be able to set up something similar with another person -- Gloster, maybe -- but if the network is already aware of the problems on Doar's turf, they could spot it and just go farther underground. And in any case, I'm guessing now that the donor intermediaries don't know inside information. Statewide there would be hundreds of them. Whoever's running the operation wouldn't make themselves vulnerable to that many people. But the candidates would be very likely to know something."

"How so?" Peter Llewellyn said.

"The candidates are receiving contributions aimed at furthering a particular set of purposes. Somebody has to coach them. Link the money to the purposes. The higher-ups wouldn't depend on simultaneous epiphany in all of their pawns."

"Maybe Doar is coaching them. Doar and the 24 others."

"Not likely. The system is elaborately set up to keep Doar as being merely a front. And there were no candidate names in the ledger, or in the Raleigh mail drop office where all the Doar documents were stored. Someone higher up is pulling the candidate strings."

"But if we go after a candidate, wouldn't that set off alarms, too?" Llewellyn said.

"We don't go after a candidate. We get someone who's already inside the system to do it," Hood said. "I'll use the dentist."

"Will he agree to do it?"

"I assure you," Hood said. "He will agree. Also, Aimee, may I ask you to penetrate the bank records? Find out what is in the accounts, and where the account statements are being mailed? The person managing the cash flow and the person pulling the strings aren't necessarily the same, but having the account details and the location of the records could be helpful."

"Meanwhile," Annie Llewellyn said, "Ames and my husband are being hunted by someone. Could we talk a little about that?"

"Yes, let's," Peter Llewellyn said. "Why not simply let them find us and tell a limited version of the truth? Ames and I are two amateurs who wanted to promote right-wing politics without being seen doing it."

"We don't have a version of that story we could sell," Hood said. "Things have gone too far. Doar tipped his hand to us by revealing the plan to elect a governor and by sending Ames to Hunter. We've tipped our hand to him with Father Llewellyn's handling of the Hunter interview, and by stealing the contents of the Fayetteville storage locker. They don't know how much we know, and they can't let that go. They have to learn who you and Ames are, what you've found out, and who you've told. I'm afraid they won't be stopped by a cooked-up story of any kind."

"So, how do we stop them?"

"They will be stopped if we can spike the statewide plan."

"That could take a long time, if we're able to do it at all. Ames and Annie and I can't hide forever. Lew can't publish The Sand Dollar out of his moving car."

"Nonetheless, for the short term we have to wait. We've

baited them with Ames' picture in The Sand Dollar, and with the theft in Fayetteville. Gloster's people are watching. If we can spot one of them, follow one of them, that might lead us to others."

"Are you sure about the truck, by the way? There's no possibility they could get into the warehouse and steal their stuff back?"

"Their stuff isn't there. Only the truck is in the warehouse. We emptied it and took the contents elsewhere."

Annie Llewellyn gestured impatience.

"I know it's difficult, Mrs. Llewellyn, "but some of our options are limited just now. We must proceed carefully. And in that connection, I must phone the dentist and then drive to Charlotte. If I leave now, I can be there by early afternoon. Meanwhile, I suggest that the rest of you take a break from all this gloomy speculation and enjoy lunch together."

Abraham Gloster rose with a flourish.

"Coming up shortly," he said. "Pulled pork barbecue, hush puppies, cole slaw and brunswick stew. I make all of it myself, and I make it better than anyone you're likely to find, if I do say so.

" I even make the sauces. Two of them. A vinegar-based sauce and a tomato-based sauce. Down in South Carolina, by the way, you'd also be offered a mustard-based sauce, which is an abomination that I won't touch. But hell, some places down in South Carolina they call brunswick stew *hash.* There's just no controlling the kind of nonsense some people will get up to."

Hood went on his way, and Gloster went to the kitchen.

"You haven't had much to say today," Peter Llewellyn said to Ames Colville.

"Been thinking."

"About what?"

"About you, actually. You can be rough as a cob sometimes."

"Meaning?"

"Are you still pissed at me? In the parking lot at Lulu's, you said that sometimes I really piss you off."

"Well, you do."

"I'm listening, Pete. I'm not ignoring you. And I'm not lazy or stupid. But it's a damn big thing to get my arms around."

"Biggest there is. Why don't you think about dropping in to some of the services at church? Be among people who've already got their arms around it, or are at least trying to. You might pick up something helpful."

"Maybe, Pete. But I'm not making any promises."

"Goddamit, Ames, I've never asked you for promises. I've just asked you to stop ducking hard questions and calling it rational. Belly up. If you decide you've been right all along, then so be it. But make a real decision."

"Well, I see I've pissed you off again."

Annie Llewellyn got her husband's attention with a hand on his arm. She gestured at Aimee, who was staring into a far corner.

"Penny for your thoughts?" Peter Llewellyn said.

"Something doesn't add up," she said.

"What doesn't?"

"The reaction is disproportionate. The Jesse Hoyt tactics. The threats. *Could have killed you. Your life would be worthless. You don't know what you've uncovered and you never will. We are everywhere.*

"What are you thinking?"

"I'm thinking you don't bring in professional criminals who threaten murder to get people elected to state offices. Not even the kind of people we've been talking about. I think something is going on here that we haven't spotted yet."

Larkin nodded agreement.

Chapter Thirty-Two

Elwood P. Hollister, D.D.S., felt important. And when he thought about it, he had to admit that he didn't often feel that way.

Yes, he was financially successful. And yes, he had a good family. And yes, he was helping the patients who came to his dental practice (although he did sometimes wonder how many would need his help if they actually did what they claimed about brushing and flossing.)

But facts were facts, and when three of the main parameters of your life were and *drill, fill and bill*, you didn't often finish a day feeling like you'd done something truly important. So, he was glad he'd agreed to cooperate when the big man pressed him to pry information out of the legislator. And he preferred to feel that he had agreed, not that the big man had made him afraid to resist.

The legislator had been glad to meet with him, for sure. Probably politicians were always glad to meet with donors, and E.P. Hollister was one of the bigger ones. The legislator had been glad to meet, and he had been pretty darned interested when E.P. told him the story that he and the big man had agreed on: With a thriving dental practice hitting a good cruising speed every day, and with more money -- frankly -- than was necessary to maintain even a pretty comfortable lifestyle, he wanted to get deeper into public service.

He wanted to expand his giving to right-minded elected officials. The community, the state and the country needed citizens who were willing to do their part. If more of them had done so, he believed, the state would not have taken some silly turns that needed to be corrected.

But he didn't want to give just willy-nilly. He wanted to be sure he was giving to right-minded men (and women, of course). And it could be pretty hard to tell where a politician would really decide to stand when the chips were down. Surely the legislator himself would agree (and he did, oh yes) that you had to be careful about choosing your politicians.

So when E.P. (please call me E.P. my friend) got on with opening his wallet, he wanted to be sure about who he was giving to. Perhaps the legislator could give him a little guidance in that regard. And yes, the legislator thought he could be helpful, if E.P. were willing to spend a little more time with him discussing ideas and policies. The legislator had some pretty strong ideas that he didn't feel free to discuss frankly in his public positions, and he knew some other people in politics who had similar views, but he didn't want to counsel E.P. on giving until he was sure they were all singing the same song, so to speak.

So they sat in the legislator's Charlotte office and chatted for quite a while, and E.P. found himself agreeing on some points that he actually had never thought about. But he was convincing, and he began to feel pretty good about the way things were going. Pretty confident, in fact. So maybe he did improvise just a bit when he moved on to part two of the theme he and the big man had agreed on: The state was in such a mess that there were lots of opportunities for course correction. No one legislator could pursue them all, and so there was ample work for all the legislator's like-minded associates to do. But how would they keep from duplicating effort? From stumbling over each other? Did they have some way of coordinating their efforts? E.P. really liked the idea of investing his money in a coordinated effort.

And that was when the legislator really got into the conversation. They had a lot to talk about, he said. Why not get away from the phones and the interruptions? Why not go to a little place out of town, across the river, that was quiet and private? It had good drinks and good food. They could take their time. Spend the evening. Make some good progress together.

Which in fact they did. With the lubrication of alcohol, the conversation got better and better. E.P. the improvisor spread his wings a little more. Like-minded people with shared goals were kind of like a team, he said. And the most successful teams had a good coach. Someone to call the signals. Did the legislator's team have a coach who called the signals? Might E.P. even meet him? He might learn a lot. If he was going to be a member of the team, he wanted to learn. He wanted to be as effective as possible.

And the legislator said he could see in E.P. a rare
opportunity that he wanted to pursue. Wanted, in fact, to pursue it
right away. Would his guest excuse him for a few minutes so that he
could make a phone call to get things under way? He didn't want to
waste any time in getting on with things.

The legislator made a couple of phone calls, in fact, and took
a couple more, and by the end of the evening -- which got to be
pretty late -- he said he had set several things up for the very next
day. If E.P. would meet him in his office first thing in the morning,
they could get going on doing good things together.

So it was that driving home with a skin full at damn near
midnight, Elwood P. Hollister, D.D.S., was feeling important. He
took the back road over the old river bridge, because almost nobody
used it anymore and the cops pretty much ignored it. He didn't want
to get caught blowing the circuits in a breathalyzer and ruin the
upcoming day. He looked forward to meeting and learning and then
telling the big man all about it.

Maybe he really would wind up being an important member
of a team -- if not the same team the legislator imagined. He was
savoring the undercover-operative feel of the thing when the
headlights showed up in his rear-view mirror. A great big bastard of
a truck, he thought, by the look of it, and barreling down on him like
a bat out of hell. Barreling right up into his rear bumper with a bang
and the screech of twisting metal.

The Cadillac fishtailed this way and that, and Elwood P.
Hollister fought the wheel, and the big bastard of a truck bore down
and smashed him again -- and again, and again.

As the concrete walls of the river bridge loomed, and he
realized that the truck was quite intentionally driving him toward
them, and he knew there was nothing he could do, he said out loud
his last conscious thought before dying in flames and wreckage.

I have been a fool.

Chapter Thirty-Three

They had Hood on speaker phone from his car.

"So," he said, "the police are treating the crash as suspicious?"

"Yes," Aimee said. "Their internal incident report leads with that note. Officers at the scene said Hollister's car sustained rear-end damage that was not consistent with a simple accident. They speculate that he was rammed and driven into the bridge wall."

"I'm very sorry to have provoked that. It represents a serious escalation. I'm afraid that even brief exposure at the newspaper office may not be safe for Mr. Perry now. Aimee, can you arrange for him to publish a few editions from our computer room at home?"

"I'm sure I can. It may be cumbersome for him, but I believe I can set it up."

Lew nodded agreement.

"And so," Hood said, "the reaction to the dentist's overture suggests that the network has been alerted to our interest. Even the candidates, or at least some of them. The people at the top are very intent on not being exposed."

"Yes, they've been alerted," Larkin said. "But now we've been alerted, too. They've revealed that they are willing to go to any extreme. And for the time being, at least, we have one advantage. They don't know who we are, or how much we know, or what our resources are."

"Yes," Hood said. "If we're careful, that should provide us a bit of safe cover for a while. But we're still no farther along toward learning the identities of the people at the top. The people pulling the strings."

"You know which legislator the dentist went to see," Peter Llewellyn said, "because you helped select him. Could you pressure him?"

"I will examine that option," Hood said. "But as I think of it, I don't expect to be able to find him. The people up the ladder will mark him as having been targeted. They will move him out of sight, I expect. We need to think of other options. Aimee, can you tell us what you discovered about the banking records?”

“The accounts don’t have much money in them at the moment. They’ve been heavily tapped.”

“That would make sense immediately after an election cycle.”

The statements go to a post office box in Raleigh. The box is rented to a George Harbison. He is 72, a retired accountant. Married, no children. He and his wife live in one of those older neighborhoods near the N.C. State campus.

“One of Gloster’s people went to the door. Pretended to be taking a survey. He said there’s a handicapped access ramp at the front entrance, and he could see one of those chair-lift mechanisms on the main staircase inside. He said that while Harbison looks to be a little on the frail side, the equipment may not be for him. He stood and walked steadily on his own. Perhaps the wife is infirm in some way.”

“Odd,” Hood said. “He doesn’t sound like someone who would be associated with people capable of murder.”

“No, he doesn’t. Nothing I could find about him suggests anything other than a lifetime solo-practice accounting business.”

“Perhaps he doesn’t fully realize who he’s dealing with.”

“Perhaps not. Should we approach him?”

“With extreme caution. If we say or do anything to alert the higher-ups, I’m afraid they will simply eliminate access in some way. Or eliminate the Harbisons themselves. From our first moment of contact, we have to give him reason to keep our visit to himself.”

“Isn’t it possible that his house is watched?”

“Yes, that is a problem.”

“Gloster’s people saw him walk to the rose garden behind the Raleigh Little Theater. He sat there for an hour reading. It could be a routine.”

“We’ll try contacting him there. It involves a certain risk nonetheless, but we’ll have to take it.”

“And if it’s not a routine? If he doesn’t go to the park every day? We don’t have a lot of time to spend waiting.”

"Then Larkin will have to enter his house surreptitiously. I would prefer to avoid alarming him in that way, but we may have no choice."

"Let's discuss how I should handle him," Larkin said.

"I propose a story that may not be far from the truth," Hood said, "except for the necessity that you tell one lie about yourself. I suggest that you pose as a federal investigator. Tell him you are looking at a criminal enterprise that funnels money through the accounts whose records he receives. Tell him that you've checked his background and are quite sure he's unaware of the nature of those activities. You can grant him immunity from prosecution, but only if he cooperates fully, from that moment forward."

"And if he says no?"

"We assume he's not really innocent, and you arrest him."

"What?"

"If he says no, we have to assume that our approach would be blown as soon as he could reach a telephone. Have one of Gloster's people standing by with a plain, late-model sedan. If you need him, signal, and put Harbison in the car. Do it quickly, so that even if you're being watched they won't have time to react. If Harbison won't cooperate with you, and you have to prevent him from reporting our contact, our best hope is simply to make him disappear mysteriously. Flash one of our counterfeit badges. That will help with your pose if they're watching."

"And what about the wife?"

"Same arrangement. Late model plain car, whisk her away. Tell her that her husband is in trouble and she needs to go to him urgently."

"Suppose she's too frail to be moved."

"Unlikely. The chair lift and the outdoor ramp suggest that she moves around the house and goes out as well."

"And what do we do with them?"

"Take them to Yaupon Bay. To our house."

"And there?"

"We'll have to improvise."

"And if the wife really is too frail to be moved?"

"She'll have to be left. Phone the Raleigh EMT service. Pose as a neighbor. Tell them she's alone in the house and needs professional help. They won't altogether understand such a call, but they won't be able to ignore it."

"This business is getting rough, Hood."

"Yes. But our options are limited, and I have a hunch that the stakes are very high. We have to find a way to link the white supremacist money more directly to the people at the top, and them to the candidates they are placing."

"And they have to find a way to provoke us to make a mistake."

"That's where we are," Hood said. "Hunters and hunted."

"And the question," Larkin said, "is which are we?"

Gloster's cell phone rang. He answered, listened briefly, and gestured for attention.

"Yes," he said. "Really? What did it say? And what did you do? Hold on, for a minute. Just hold on."

Gloster turned toward the speaker phone.

"Can you hear me, Hood?"

"Yes."

"There's been a development. My people watching the newspaper office saw a man approach and nail something to the door. It was a clipping from the Fayetteville Observer. This morning's edition. The story said that the man in Fayetteville had been murdered. The one who ran the storage place. There was a note scrawled by hand on the clipping. It said, 'Your move, John Smith.' "

"Did they get a tag number or anything we can use to track him down?"

"Don't need to. They grabbed him. They're on the phone right now asking me what they should do with him."

"Good heavens. Tell them to blindfold him and bring him to you there at our house."

"What do I do with him then?"

"Put him in the runabout and take him to our shack in The Barren. Give him food and water for overnight. I will be home tonight and deal with him tomorrow. You can still make it to Raleigh tonight and deal with Harbison tomorrow.”

“Tomorrow is shaping up to be an eventful day.”

“Indeed. And when you leave our hostage in The Barren?”

“Yes.”

“Warn him not to go outdoors at night. I want him to be fit to deal with when I pick him up.”

Chapter Thirty-Four

Larkin strolled the perimeter of the rose garden; paused and pretended to watch a wedding rehearsal in the amphitheater; stole sidelong glances at Harbison on his bench.

To help the appearance of coincidental meeting, he'd given Harbison a good half hour to read. He moved to the bench, sat and nodded hello. Harbison looked up from his book and returned the nod.

Larkin timed five minutes before he spoke.

"Nice day to sit in the sun."

Harbison looked up, nodded, returned to his book.

"Early November is often a good time for it. Not too hot, not too cold. Not really wintertime yet."

Harbison looked up again, held eye contact.

"For your personal safety and your wife's, Mr. Harbison, you must pretend that we are chatting about the weather and the rose bushes."

Larkin swept his hand in a gesture at the garden.

"I am a federal law enforcement officer. I am going to reach into my coat for a handkerchief. When I lift my lapel, you will be able to see my badge. Don't stare, please."

Larkin produced a handkerchief, cleaned an imaginary spot on the bench, returned the handkerchief.

Harbison closed his hook, painted on a smile, turned to hook an elbow over the back of the bench.

"Go on," he said.

"We are investigating a criminal enterprise that funnels money through certain bank accounts. The statements on those accounts are mailed to a post office box rented in your name. We have investigated your background, and we are satisfied that you are unaware of the full nature of the enterprise. But the fact remains, you are a participant in its operation. I can offer you immunity from prosecution in return for your help. However, our investigation is moving quite rapidly, and I must have your answer immediately. Right now."

Harbison paused a beat.

"Alright," he said. "How can I help?"

"Tell me in detail what you do."

"The statements arrive at the box on a staggered schedule. I collect them and take them home."

"Do you open them?"

"Never."

"Why not?"

"I am persuaded that doing so would be very unwise."

"What happens to them?"

"I bundle them. Four times a month, just before bedtime, I put them in the mailbox beside my front door. When I get up the next morning they are gone."

"Where do they go?"

"I don't know."

"Who collects them?"

"I don't know."

"How long have you been doing this?"

"Two years."

"Are you paid?"

"Yes."

"How?"

"In cash. They leave it in my mailbox when they pick up the statements."

"How much?"

"One thousand dollars a month."

"Always on time?"

"Always."

"Tell me how it started."

"A young man came to our house. He was very well turned out. Expensive suit, expensive shoes, expensive haircut. He was pleasant and smooth, except that he had the eyes of a snake. He offered me ten thousand dollars to rent the box and let them use it. Put the cash right in my hand, right then and there. Promised the weekly payment if I would clear the box and bring the statements to my house."

"Who is 'them'?"

"He didn't say, I didn't ask."

"What was his name?"

"He didn't say, I didn't ask."

Larkin turned toward the wedding rehearsal.

"Young people beginning a life," he said.

"Yes," Harbison said. "I envy them."

Larkin turned back.

"Mr. Harbison, you must realize that your story is very odd. A stranger comes to your house and offers you a great deal of money to do very little. You accept the arrangement without even knowing his name. You cannot possibly have thought that the enterprise was legitimate."

"I didn't care."

"Why did you do it?"

"My wife is ill. Parkinson's. We have been together for 50 years. Perhaps you've read about marriages in which two people really become one? That's us. I was deeply troubled by her suffering. I wanted to do what I could to ease it as much as possible. I have used the money to give her a little bit more of a life for as long as I can."

"But surely you knew that it couldn't last. The money."

"I assumed it would not, but I wanted to collect it as long as I could."

"And so, you are not terribly surprised by this conversation."

"Not terribly, no."

"And I must say that you don't seem very troubled by it, either. By the prospect of losing the money."

"I would have lost it anyway. No matter what you or they or others did. I am terminally ill. Cancer. Which means, by the way, that you needn't bother with any paperwork or administrative detail that would be involved in arranging immunity from prosecution. I don't have long. By the time anyone could bring me to trial, I would be dead."

"I am very sorry."

"So am I. But I've done what I could. In the time I have left, what do you want of me? What do you want me to do?"

"Nothing."

"Nothing?"

"Don't change your behavior. Keep right on as you have been. We will handle the rest."

"May I keep taking the money?"

"Yes."

"Will you take it away from my wife later?"

"No."

"That is a very odd thing for a federal law enforcement agent to allow."

"Consider it part of the immunity deal."

Harbison's smile became genuine.

"May I ask one question?"

"Certainly."

"How do you suppose they picked me?"

"I'd be guessing."

"Please do."

"They wanted someone who was desperate enough to accept the deal."

"Well, they got that part right."

"Scams on the elderly are commonplace nowadays. People like this would know people who were involved in that kind of thing. They would have means of spotting elderly targets. By one means or another, you turned up in the pool."

"I see. May I ask one more question?"

"Of course."

"Are you really a federal agent?"

Larkin smiled but didn't answer.

"I guess it really doesn't really matter much at this point, does it?" Harbison said.

"No," Larkin said. "Godspeed, Mr. Harbison. We will keep you safe."

Chapter Thirty-Five

"So, you couldn't find the legislator who met with the dentist," Gloster said.

"No," Aimee said. "As Hood suspected, he's disappeared. Vacationing in Europe, according to his office."

"And Hood is with the other guy now? The one my people nabbed at the newspaper office?"

"Yes. They are talking in a back room."

"I thought I heard an unusual sound. Right after I got here. It sounded a little like, I don't know, like wind, maybe."

"Yes. You did. Here they come."

With a grip on his upper arm, Hood led the dazed hostage into the living room.

"Sit," Hood said.

The hostage flinched and sat.

"Be still. Don't move," Hood said.

At the sound of Hood's voice, the hostage flinched again. His hands shook. He clasped them to still them.

Hood himself sank into a chair. He passed a hand over his face, drew a deep breath and looked up at the group.

"Jesse Hoyt isn't a person," he said. "Strictly speaking, it isn't even an alias. It's an organization. It's built on a sort of business model. There is a national group. A core, so to speak, with its own people. Some of the organization's work is done by them. Other kinds of work they franchise out to local people on an ad-hoc basis. They keep the work and the working relationships highly compartmentalized. Only people at the very top have anything like a total picture. Everyone else knows only what his own job is. He may be assigned to work with others, or he may work alone. If he works with others, each knows only his own part in the job at hand. Locals may be supervised by someone from the core group, or they may work on their own."

"I'm guessing this guy is a local," Gloster said.

"Yes."

"And he worked on his own?"

"Yes."

"Does he know who hired him?"

"No. He's worked for them before, and the pattern is always the same. He gets his assignment in a phone call. He does the job, and a cash deposit appears in his bank account."

"This Jesse Hoyt thing is a goddamn Hydra," Gloster said. "Even if we could keep baiting them into the open, we might be wasting time with drones."

"Exactly so," Hood said.

"Do we know what Larkin learned in Raleigh?" Gloster said.

"Not yet," Aimee said. "He's on his way back. He should be here within the hour."

"Unless he got something big, we're not much farther along. We need some way to break through to the top. I'd give a lot to know who their candidate is -- the one they're going to put up for governor."

"I'm not sure that would matter much," Aimee said.

"What?"

Aimee turned to the hostage.

"What's your phone number?"

He gave her a dazed puzzled look.

"What's your phone number?"

He croaked out an answer.

Aimee opened a file and tapped a forefinger in the middle of the top page.

"Yes. It's here."

Hood raised his eyebrows with a question.

"Something's been bothering me for a while," Aimee said. "Something's just not quite right. It started with this list we got from the storage place. It's supposed to be a list of people who had something stored in the explosives locker. Look at it. The Jesse Hoyt name is at the top. Just the name. Nothing else. All the other names had addresses and phone numbers.

"OK, so Jesse Hoyt is an alias. An alias doesn't have a phone number, and someone using an alias doesn't tell you how to reach them at home. So far, so good. But it doesn't answer my question. Why this particular list? What does professional criminal muscle have in common with a bunch of racist has-beens? Nothing. Does he want their guns and explosives? Not a chance. They were collected by amateurs. They could be traceable in a dozen ways.

"So, finding the Jesse Hoyt name on this list is like finding a grape in a box of raisins.
Now, all the other names and addresses checked out. They are real people who live or work at those addresses. But the first time around, I didn't bother with the phone numbers. The grape thing still troubled me. So, I went back and checked out the phone numbers. They don't match. Not a one of them is really the phone number of the listed person. This number here on the list is his."

She gestured at the hostage.

"Think about it. If you're a Jesse Hoyt operative, and you need a little job done in Yaupon Bay, and you want local help, how do you locate the help? You can't place a want ad. You have to know where to find it. Your organization has to have told you where to find it. This list isn't a customer inventory for a storage locker. It's a directory of Jesse Hoyt henchmen in eastern North Carolina."

Gloster whistled

Lew Perry murmured, "Good God."

Hood smiled.

"And then I was bothered by the extreme nature of the reactions to our efforts. Two people have been murdered. Three have disappeared, including one state legislator. This is big-time behavior. It's exactly the kind of thing the federal people identify with the Jess Hoyt alias. And now we find that's a major criminal organization. But what would that kind have in common with a bunch of white supremacist politicians? Again, the answer is nothing. That kind of organization doesn't care about white supremacy or any other kind of ideology. It cares about making money -- a lot more than it can make by skimming contributions from over-the-hill neo-Nazis."

Hood's smile grew.

"And your conclusion is?" he said

"We've been looking at things upside down. We supposed the crooks were working for the politicians. I think it's the opposite. I think the politicians are working for the crooks. It's well disguised.

The camouflage is two layers deep. Garden variety conservative causes on the surface. White supremacy one layer down for the folks who are really cranked up. And the truth underneath is plain old-fashioned corruption. The crooks don't care about the politics of it. They don't have to succeed in taking over the legislature, or that kind of thing. They just need camouflage for sneaking some of their people into key positions. The possibilities are huge. Money laundering through state agencies. Corruption of law enforcement. Doar talked from the first about packing the judiciary. So if you look at it this way, the identity of the gubernatorial candidate, for example, doesn't matter hugely. He or she would just be a puppet. Same could go for the string-puller running the political bag-money operation. Just another puppet."

Hood rocked back in his chair.

"Organized crime," he murmured. "Phenix City Alabama on a statewide scale. Good heavens."

Lew Perry's cell phone rang. He stepped out of the room to take the call.

"We'll need to change our thinking completely," Hood said.

"I hope Larkin got something good in Raleigh," Gloster said. "I don't like this feeling of being stymied."

Lew returned and gestured for attention.

"A contact in the police department," he said. "Watches the daily reports and lets me know what's up. Lulu has been killed."

"Robbery?" Ames Colville said.

"No. Murder. Execution, actually. She was tied to a chair and beaten to death."

Peter Llewellyn heaved an agonized groan and buried his face in his hands.

"I told Hunter's goon that Lulu was my sister. I just blurted it out on the spur of the moment. I got that woman killed."

The rest of the group fell silent. Peter Llewellyn's head snapped up.

"And I've done it twice. The Wakefield family. These people will connect the Wakefield family to me."

"How? Gloster said.

"That thing Sunday at church. The guy gave Billy the message to be hand-delivered to me. He knew I was still there. He looked in the parish hall and saw me. You were with me, Hood. And Larkin and Aimee. He'd already spotted you as being involved with me in the Doar business. The only other people in the room were the Wakefields. We were having a discussion. A serious one. The guy had no way of knowing that it was on a completely different subject from the Doar business."

"But he wouldn't know who the Wakefields are," Gloster said.

"The church directory. It's online, and it's illustrated."

"Damn," Hood said. "They could have been harmed already."

"No," Peter Llewellyn said. "They are away. After the crisis at the fire station, they took Billy away for a while, to let him settle down and have some peaceful time. They left immediately."

"When are they due back?"

"Today. Tonight, actually."

"The Hoyt people could easily know that," Hood said. "An automatic *we're-away* message on voicemail or email. Failing that, there are other ways. *Hello? Is this the newspaper circulation department? My name is William Wakefield. I'm on vacation, and I don't remember if I asked you to suspend delivery of my paper. Could you check that? I did? And what do your records say about when to resume delivery? Yes. That's correct. Thanks.*"

"We have to get to the Wakefield house," Hood said.

"I hear daddy's car in the yard," Aimee said.

"Aimee, I'd like you to come with us as backup. Father Llewellyn, do you have Mr. Wakefield's cell phone number?"

"Yes."

"I want you to call him. Keep calling him until you get through. Tell him that he must not for any reason go to his house until he hears from us again."

"Annie can do that. I'm going with you."

"No, please."

"Fuck off, Hood. I'm responsible for putting that little family in danger. I'm going to be there. I'll go with you, or I'll follow you. Your choice. You have no other."

"This could be very rough, Father Llewellyn."

“I can handle myself.”

“Alright. Let’s get ready. We should leave as soon as possible.

Chapter Thirty-Six

The Wakefields' block was bisected end-to-end by a narrow alley that served each house from the rear. In gathering darkness, the four of them crouched between the back wall of the Wakefields' garage and a six-foot alley fence.

"Mrs. Llewellyn was not able to reach the Wakefields?" Hood said.

"No," Aimee said. "My guess is that they are driving home. Cell phones off in the car."

"Not good," Hood said. "They could show up at any moment. We could wind up dealing with the Hoyt people and the Wakefields all at the same time."

"Then we'd better get moving," Larkin said. "I'll check the situation again."

He laid aside a short-barreled, pistol grip shotgun. Hood wore a nine-millimeter pistol under his left arm, and another at the small of his back with the grip turned toward his left side. Between his shoulder blades he wore a scabbard with four balanced throwing knives. Aimee wore a nine-millimeter pistol holstered on her right hip. On her left hip she wore a pair of nunchaku. Llewellyn was unarmed, but dressed for action in loose dark clothes and athletic shoes.

They watched Larkin ghost across the yard and around the perimeter of the house. For a time, he was out of sight. He silently re-appeared at the rear corner of the garage. One moment he was nowhere to be seen, and the next moment he was moving in beside them.

"It's as I said before," Larkin said.

"Let's review, please," Hood said.

"There are three of them. Their attention is focused toward the front of the house. The garage is full of lawn equipment and storage items. The Wakefields don't use it for their car. The three Hoyt men are calculating that the Wakefields will park in the driveway and use the front entrance.

"The hallway runs through the center of the house from front to back. Facing forward from the back of the house, we'll see a living room front left, a dining room front right. A small bedroom and guest bath open off the hallway on the left. Two other bedrooms open off the hallway on the right. The kitchen spans the back.

"The Wakefields left timer controls on several lights. The Hoyt men do not appear to have tampered with them, so that the house would appear normal to the Wakefields from the outside. All three men are armed with handguns. All three handguns are holstered at the moment.

"All three men are seated for now. Man one is against the front wall of the living room at the left edge of the picture window. The blinds on the picture window are drawn, but he can see the driveway by looking through the side.

"Man two is at the left rear corner of the living room. He has a clear line of sight to the front door. Man three is seated in the doorway between the living room and dining room. When the front door is opened, he will be out of sight behind it.

"They are estimating that the Wakefields will either enter the room without noticing anything, because their attention will be focused on luggage and each other; or, that the Wakefields will notice man two in the far corner and focus their attention there long enough for man one and man three to herd them on into the house.

"Your recommendation on tactics?" Hood said.

"The back kitchen door lock is flimsy. I can easily disable it without making sound. We should be able to reach the rear threshold of the living room without being detected. I will vault the sofa and immobilize man one. Hood, as soon as I move, you can step into the room and use a throwing knife to immobilize man two. The movement -- and I'm sure noise from man two -- will attract the attention of man three. Aimee, you should be able to reach and immobilize him with time to spare. Mr. Llewellyn, you can follow us in and help out if any of them get foolishly unruly."

"I'm going in with the first three," Llewellyn snapped.

"Please now, no," Hood said.

"I got this little family in trouble by deciding to mix into this business in the first place. I am not going to sit out here and pick my nose while the rest of you clean up my mess. I'm going in with the first three. I'll go in as part of a plan, if you'll cooperate, or I'll just go in when I get good and ready."

"You'll be dealing with armed men," Hood said.

"I've dealt with armed men before," Llewellyn snarled. "When I finished dealing with them, they weren't armed anymore."

"You're angry," Hood said.

"You're goddamn right I'm angry."

"Angry can be treacherous in a tactical situation."

"Too damn bad. I'm not sitting on my ass through this one."

Hood looked questions at Larkin and Aimee. They shrugged acquiescence.

Hood nodded at Larkin.

"Alright," Larkin said. "Let's do it this way. I will go with man one, as I said before, and

Hood with man two. Llewellyn will take man three. But I still don't like his being armed and you not. Aimee, please follow closely to deal with any difficulties."

"Speaking of difficulties," Aimee said, "it's been several minutes since you assessed the scene. Suppose they've changed position or something when we go in?"

"We will have to improvise," Larkin said. "I will make the first choice of target, Hood the second, Llewellyn the third with you close behind."

He reached out, grabbed the front of Llewellyn's shirt and pulled him in so that they were nose to nose.

"You are taking bullheaded risks here, with our lives as well as yours, Mr. Preacher Llewellyn. If you fuck up, my daughter or my son-in-law could be injured or killed. In any such event, what happens to them will happen to you. I will see to it."

Llewellyn opened his mouth to respond.

"Shut up," Larkin said, pushing him back. "You've talked enough tonight."

He rose and made for the house. The other three followed closely.

With Larkin in the lead, they reached the threshold of the living room undetected. The Hoyt men had not moved. Larkin glanced over his shoulder. Hood nodded. Larkin whirled into the room, vaulted the back of a sofa and shoved the shotgun muzzle under the chin of man one.

"Short barrel. Heavy load. You'd be headless," he murmured in man one's ear.

Hood pivoted toward man two, who was rising and reaching for his weapon. Hood put a throwing knife through the bicep of his gun hand, and another through the thigh of his right leg, just above the knee. Man two cried out and went down.

Man three was confused and distracted by the simultaneous action in two separate corners of the room. Llewellyn reached him as he fumbled to pull his gun. With a savage right hook, Llewellyn bounced his head off the door jam. He tore man three's gun away and hurled it down the hall. With two hands, he seized man three by the throat and lifted his feet off the floor.

Llewellyn smashed man three's head against the door jam. Smashed it again. And again. Man three pummeled and twisted and kicked. Llewellyn smashed again. And again.

Even after man three went limp, Llewellyn smashed him against the door jam. He smashed until he heard Billy Wakefield calling …

"Father Pete! Father Pete!"

He turned to see the front door standing open and Aimee using outstretched arms to keep the wide-eyed Wakefield family from walking into the scene.

Llewellyn looked into the living room and saw that even Hood and Larkin were staring at him.

Chapter Thirty-Seven

"Damn fine spread," Gloster said to Aimee. Don't think I've ever seen a breakfast like it."

"Hood wanted to gather early," Aimee said. "He feels we may have a lot to think about today. He likes being a good host, and he enjoys the cooking."

"Where are the three guys you brought home from the Wakefields' house?"

"They are on the island in The Barren with the first one. Hood wants them to have some time together. He thinks two or three days out there in the swamp may loosen their tongues -- first with each other. He wants the first man to have time to tell the new three about his experience here. He thinks that after a while they may decide to break the compartmentalization rules and tell each other what they know. After they've told each other, they could be persuaded to tell us."

"What did happen to that first guy? He acted like his brains had been rattled."

"Before this is over you may well get a chance to see for yourself. Look. Here come the Wakefields."

"My goodness," Sarah Jane Wakefield said. "What is all this?"

"Breakfast," Aimee said. "Take your choice. We have various juices. All the standard ones plus beet-lemon and carrot-ginger, which are much better than they sound. We can make a variety of omelets. Also eggs benedict, crab cakes benedict, eggs Florentine. Or you can have pancakes, Belgian waffles, French toast. There is an acai berry bowl, and avocado toast. Also, an assortment of pastries. Coffee and a variety of teas, as you like."

"Do you have Captain Crunch?" Billy Wakefield said.

"Billy, I'm very sorry, we don't. But I bet we can find something you like. How about some of those sticky buns over there."

"Wow. Those look good."

The group showed up in ones and twos, filled plates and scattered around the open living room to eat at quiet leisure.

Hood and Larkin cleaned up piecemeal as they finished.

Aimee chatted with Billy.

"Did you see the boat out back?" she said.

"Yes ma'am. It looks way cool."

"Maybe you and your dad would like to take it out for a ride? We have some fishing poles and things."

"Oh, wow. Could we, Dad?"

Aimee shot Bill Wakefield a long look.

"We have some talking to do," she said.

She flicked a glance at Billy.

"I understand," Bill Wakefield said.

"You comfortable handling the boat?"

"Completely."

"When you reach the mouth of the creek, go left down to the bay. If you go right, you'll go into The Barren. You don't want that. You'll have no trouble coming back. The mouth of the creek is marked."

"Come on sport," Bill Wakefield said. "Let's get some gear together."

"I'll stay here with Ivy," Sarah Jane Wakefield said. "Then I can bring Bill up to date when he and Billy get back."

"Good," Aimee said.

"Let's gather and take stock," Hood said when everyone had finished eating. "Bring your beverages."

They gathered in the circle of chairs.

"As I see it," Hood said, "we have two main avenues of approach. One is through the three men we brought here last night. Unfortunately, that one requires us first to wait a bit. We need for the reality of their situation to settle in on them. The other avenue, I hope, lies with what Larkin learned in Raleigh. Can you fill us in?"

"Yes. The headline is that the Harbisons are elderly, ill and essentially innocent. He is terminal. He is paid cash to clear the post office box and turn the contents over to a courier. That's all. He is aware that he is probably involved in shady dealings, but he estimates that he will die before he can be punished, and in the meantime the money helps his wife."

"How does the handoff occur?" Hood asked. "To the courier."

"Harbison places the material -- at night -- in the mailbox on his front porch. The next morning it's gone."

"The obvious first option is to follow the courier," Hood said. "The downside of that is that doing so might be a waste of time. It's unlikely that a courier reports directly to the top of the organization. We could be facing a chain of intermediaries. Or it's possible that the courier doesn't actually go anywhere. He could simply re-package the material and put it back in the mail to another destination.

"An alternative would be to capture the courier and sweat him. But that would quite certainly endanger the Harbisons and, again, might well only tell us that the courier knows little or nothing. I simply can't see a path that doesn't keep us in the position of taking small steps, when what we need is a breakthrough of some sort."

With murmurs, nods and frowns, the group agreed.

"May I offer an idea?" Annie Llewellyn said.

"Certainly."

"Cut off the money."

"Pardon?"

"Cut off the money. Larkin has already gained access to that Raleigh room full of signed blank checks. Aimee has already determined the balances in the bank accounts. Go to Raleigh and steal enough checks to empty the accounts. The checks are valid, the signatures are valid. Take the money and contribute it to the ACLU or the Southern Poverty Law Center."

Larkin murmured in appreciation.

"Meanwhile," Annie continued, "you intercept the courier and stop delivery of the bank statements. Bribe him, threaten him, do whatever it takes. If the statements suddenly stop coming, they'll soon check the accounts and find them empty. They won't send an underling to deal with that kind of thing."

"We would have to undertake protection of the Harbisons," Hood said, "but for a major breakthrough it would be worthwhile doing."

"We could rent a beach house for the Harbisons, the Wakefields and the Llewellyns," Aimee said. "Houses would be available. The tourist season is over. There would be the problem of Billy's school work, but I'm sure we could arrange computer access to his lesson plans. He could be home-tutored for a time."

"Mrs. Llewellyn," Hood said, "you have just the felonious streak we need at the moment. Many thanks."

Annie Llewellyn grinned.

"I propose that we proceed as follows," Hood said. "I will ask the Wakefields and the Llewellyns to arrange for a beach house. We will bear the cost. Any facility that you feel is appropriate will be fine. Gloster can help with logistics. He is able to move more freely than the rest of you. And may I ask you, Father Llewellyn -- may I implore you -- to reconsider holding your Sunday services personally? Surely now you would be willing to let someone fill in."

Peter Llewellyn looked at the floor.

"Yes," he murmured. "I will make that arrangement."

"Aimee, Larkin and I will go to Raleigh. We will steal the checks, arrange to move the Harbisons, and deal with the courier."

With nods and murmurs, the group agreed.

"Let's get to work," Hood said.

As the group began to disperse, Sarah Jane Wakefield put a hand on Aimee's arm.

"Two of the three men you took from our house were wounded," she said.

"Larkin patched them up," Aimee said. "They'll have some pain, but they'll survive."

"Larkin is trained for that?"

"Experienced," Aimee said.

Peter Llewellyn looked at the floor and said nothing.

Chapter Thirty-Eight

On the oceanfront deck of the rental house, Lillian Harbison adjusted her lap blanket and scanned the vista with bright eyes.

"I knew it was funny money," she said to Aimee, without taking her gaze off the view.

"Pardon?"

"The money George had all of a sudden to do things for me. This chair. It does everything but talk. The chair lift at home. George has worked hard all his life, and we've always had a comfortable income. But suddenly there was cash for extras. And all the extras were for me. I knew it had to be funny money. I knew but didn't ask."

"You didn't want to know?"

"He wouldn't have answered. He would have kissed my cheek and changed the subject. George is very sweet and very protective. From the very beginning in our marriage, if there was a situation he thought might worry me, and he was sure he could handle it himself, he would just hide it. If I suspected, and if I asked, he just kissed me on the cheek and changed the subject. I learned early on that it was a loving gesture, and I should just accept it. I always have, and I've never regretted it. So, I didn't ask."

Billy Wakefield popped up from a ground floor patio.

"Mr. Gloster wants to know do you want a burger or a dog," he said to Lillian Harbison. "And whichever it is, how do you want it? And do you want iced tea with it? He says to tell you that you've never tasted iced tea like his."

"Well, young Mr. Wakefield, would you please tell Mr. Gloster that I want a burger and two dogs. Tell him I'd like chili on the dogs and lettuce and tomato on the burger. Also, please tell him not to cook all the life out of the burger. And with all due respect to his iced tea, I'd like a beer."

"Yes ma'am."

"Nice boy," Lillian Harbison said.

"Yes, he is."

"I gather he's dealing with some issues?"

"He's seen some things that boys shouldn't have to deal with. But he has great parents. They're working on it."

"Tell me about all these people. Are they your friends?"

"Friends and acquaintances. We're trying to help some of them. Others are trying to help us help."

"Who are those two over there?"

"The older one owns the local weekly newspaper. The younger one works for him. They are finishing up a story."

"Must be a good one. They look intense."

"A Charlotte law firm was fronting quiet land purchases north of town. Those two wanted to know why. The lawyers gave them a line about a big commercial development that would mean jobs for the town. But something was fishy. They kept poking into it. Turned out that one of the law partners was a specialist in getting around environmental regulations. Their client was secretly applying for state permits to build a landfill."

"Are they helpers or helped?"

"Some of both. We started out pursuing something else and wound up getting the Llewellyns in trouble with a gang of criminals. Long story."

"And this fellow Gloster?"

"He showed up unexpectedly. He's a college teacher up in Charlotte. He also undertakes to keep track of right-wing troublemakers. There is some overlap there with the gang activity. Again, it's a long story."

"This man Hood. He is your husband?"

"Yes."

"And Larkin is your father?"

"Yes."

"They are good men? Good human beings?"

"Yes."

"Why are you doing all this? Why are you helping us?"

"We are lucky to have a bit of money and some skills. We try to help people when we can."

"You do this as a business?"

"No. Sometimes we ask for a fee, but we took this one pro bono."

Lillian Harbison let her inquiry drop. She and Aimee sat silent, watching the ocean and listening to the sound of group lunch-making on the patio below.

George Harbison came into view on the beach, rounding a high dune and pushing head-down into a steady breeze.

"He's dying, you know. My George," Lillian Harbison said.

"Yes, I know. He seems to be very brave about it. Is he in pain?"

"Not yet."

"May I ask about his prognosis? How long does he have?"

"Depends on which doctor you ask and what his favored mode of treatment is. Maybe a year, maybe a little longer. But of course, when all is said and done it's a total dice roll. George devotes every day to doing as well as he can at being George. And my George is a pretty good guy for anyone to be."

The two of them fell silent again. George Harbison made his way up from the beach and joined the lunch-fixing group on the patio.

At length, Lillian Harbison said, "Are they very bad men?"

"Who?"

"These criminals who are troubling the Llewellyns."

"Yes, I'm afraid they are very bad men."

"What do they do?"

"A lot of things."

"Do they steal?"

"Yes."

"Do they kill people?"

"Yes, they have."

"How did you get involved with this?"

"We stumbled across them. We discovered they were trying to put people in state government and use them to grow their enterprises."

"And these are the people who paid us the funny money?"

"Yes."

"Did we do a terrible thing, George and I, taking the money?"

"Not really. They only wanted courier service. They would have found someone in any case."

"What exactly did George do for them?"

"He forwarded mail."

"That's all?"

"Yes."

"What was in the mail?"

"Bank statements."

"Nothing more?"

"Nothing."

"And you brought us here because …?"

"We intercepted delivery of the bank statements. The crooks would then know that you had revealed your role to third parties."

"And they would have retaliated against us?"

"In all likelihood they would have killed you."

Lillian Harbison turned to Aimee with a steady, unruffled gaze.

"Well then, young lady, let me say that I hope you and yours are fully competent at what you do. Even given our age and circumstances, George and I would regret dying before our time."

She finished off with a small chuckle and turned back to the view.

Hood came up from the patio.

"Gloster's people called," he said. "There's been another contact. Another note tacked to the office door at The Sand Dollar."

"Did they grab another courier?" Aimee said.

"No. This one was accompanied by four armed men. They were out of their car and back into it in 60 seconds."

"What did the note say?"

" 'We should meet.' It gave a phone number."

Chapter Thirty-Nine

"You're not John Smith," the operative said as Hood slipped into the booth.

"And you're not Jesse Hoyt, because there is no person named Jesse Hoyt. So let's skip the tap dancing with each other. In fact, let's order lunch, so the server will go away and we can talk."

Both picked Lil's fried lunch platter. Flounder, shrimp and clam strips with coleslaw, hushpuppies and sweet iced tea.

"You have taken several of our people," the operative said.

"Yes."

"And apparently they have revealed information to you."

"Yes. I can be very persuasive."

" Are they alive?"

"Yes."

"Are they in good condition?"

"Depends on your point of view."

The operative gave Hood an appraising look and focused on his food for a time.

"You have some of our money," he finally said.

"No, we don't have it."

"You are the ones who stole it."

"Yes, we did. But we don't have it. We gave it away."

The operative appraised Hood again.

"Who is *we*?"

"Partners and associates. People who like their privacy."

"And who are you?"

"We are all businessmen, like yourselves."

"Why are you interfering with us?"

"I would say it's the other way around."

"How so?"

"You are outsiders on our turf. You are complicating our operations and raising our operating costs."

"How did you find out about us?"

"You left tracks, and we are very good at our business. We are very good at yours, too."

"You can't defeat us, no matter who you are and how good you are. We are everywhere."

"We can make your life complicated enough to bring you here seeking some kind of relief."

"True. True enough. What do you want?"

"Ideally, I would like you to get off my turf."

"No. We view it as our turf."

"Well, if you're not leaving and we're not leaving, then perhaps it's necessary to talk about collaboration. Some kind of partnership."

"We might be willing to discuss an arrangement. What exactly did you have in mind?"

"Details I'll discuss only with people at the top, and that's not you."

"What makes you think so?"

"Can you make commitments? Right here, right now?"

"No."

"That's what makes me think so. Tell your bosses that I'm the person at the top for us. I will only negotiate with counterparts on your side. No more errand boys."

The operative rose and curled his lip.

"You're an arrogant sonovabitch."

"I practice."

"If we decide to talk more, how will we contact you?"

"Tack another note on the door. And tell your bosses they don't have to bother with the armed guards from now on. We've already found out that we don't learn much from errand boys. Witness this lunch."

The operative wheeled away.

"Oh, and by the way," Hood called after him. "Lunch is on me. No thanks necessary."

Larkin and Aimee waited five minutes before slipping into the booth with Hood.

"Did you succeed in rattling his cage?" Larkin said.

"Maybe. And he said something interesting. I'm not sure he was aware of it, but he said something very interesting."

"What?"

"He used the same phrase as the intruder at the church: 'We are everywhere.' "

"What are you thinking?"

"We already knew that their operation is statewide, or aims to be. I'm thinking of that list of names and phone numbers on the computer at the Fayetteville storage business. The directory of local talent for hire. They can't have that kind of information scattered at random all over the state. Someone has to know where all of it is, so that operatives can be directed to it.
Somebody has the master list, and somebody uses it to send regional lists to outposts like the Fayetteville storage place."

"And that," Larkin said, "would logically be someone at the top of the organization."

"Precisely. Aimee? That spying software you put on the Fayetteville computer. Is it still there? It doesn't self-destruct after a time?"

"It's still there."

"Could you use it to find the source of that directory? The location of the computer that sent the directory to Fayetteville?"

"Why yes, I think so."

"I believe we have just gained the advantage of surprise."

Chapter Forty

No one ever compiled a complete picture of the denouement. The component parts of it were scattered across hundreds of miles of geography and multiple layers of government and law enforcement.

Dennis Eastman, editor of The Watauga Free Press, glimpsed the heart of it unawares in one of his monthly coffees with Sheriff W.T. "Buck" Buckminster. For 20 years the two had maintained a wary friendship in keeping with the tenor of their very first transaction:

Buckminster: "I don't like to see half-assed shit in the newspaper."

Eastman: "I don't like to put half-assed shit in the newspaper, so I guess you I won't have any problems as long as we're straight with each other."

For the most part, their coffee talk focused on hunting, fishing, sports and politics. But occasionally one would offer the other a friendly nudge away from a false trail or bad information. The nudges might be camouflaged. Like an old married couple, they had their signs and signals. But each recognized and valued them.

"Buck," Eastman said. "I've got to ask you some things straight out about the Cherokee Forest murder."

"Off the record?"

"Yes. Off the record."

"Ask what you like. Maybe I'll answer, maybe I won't."

"I hear the state and federal people have pretty much taken over the investigation."

"Pretty much."

"Why have they hushed up the cause of death?"

"What makes you ask?"

"Come on, Buck. Guy owns a 50-acre estate on the edge of a national forest? That's major money. Rumors of Miami mob ties? That's major crime, way up here in the mountains. Four so-called household staff drugged with dart guns, bound and stacked up like cordwood? The big guy himself dead as a mackerel, and the only thing missing is one computer? That's the biggest story in years. So, why the lid on the cause of death?"

"They're embarrassed. They don't know the cause of death."

"How the hell could they not know the cause of death?"

"Medical examiner says he's never seen the like of it. Says the nearest he can come to describing it is that the guy was frightened to death."

***   ***
***

Law enforcement agencies in South Florida began receiving anonymous tips about the whereabouts of mob money, mob drugs, mob hideouts, mob plans and mob corpses. Resulting operations crippled major enterprises of organized crime from Miami to Atlanta. Budding plans to reach north into the Carolinas and Virginia were extinguished.

Eager to publicize these results, but not eager to confess their anonymous provenance, law enforcement officials attributed their successes to "the bravery and hard work of dedicated investigators." Eager to share in the glory, and therefore not eager to look gift horses in the mouth, higher-ups did not press questions.

***   ***
***

A veteran political operator in North Carolina abruptly announced his retirement from the field. Observers were shocked by his abandonment of a hugely successful career in campaign management and fund-raising. They were doubly shocked by his announcement of a call to missionary service, as all his previous expressions of reverence had been focused on power and money.

Curious reporters pursued the story. Some tried to establish a connection between the operator and a little-publicized organization called Restore Our State, which had suddenly dried up.

207

The operator denied any connection with a vehemence that was itself the subject of media speculation.

Eight state legislators and three announced candidates also resigned, citing a variety of time-of-life urges to pursue other interests. A state senator who had visibly flirted with gubernatorial aspirations began denying that any such notion had ever occurred to him.

Curious reporters pursued the stories. They found nothing, and eventually moved on to other matters.

***   ***
***

Abraham Gloster's people compiled a dossier from information gathered at Marvin Penny's white supremacy rally: License plate numbers, surreptitious photographs, overheard conversations.

One particularly enterprising volunteer scouted the peripheral tree line and photographed a couple acrobatically in flagrante. Deducing that they were married -- but not to each other -- the volunteer proposed blackmail in furtherance of the higher cause. Gloster made him destroy the photos.

Other dossiers were compiled from the records of Daniel Doar's 24 colleagues in campaign contribution laundering. These were combined with records of bank deposits from the Raleigh document repository of Restore Our State.

Campaign donor intermediaries began receiving anonymous mailings of cash-flow charts. Most of the donors eschewed further interest in politics.

Elwood P. Hollister's widow received a large windfall in a check drawn on an account in the name of Restore Our State.

***   ***
***

George and Lillian Harbison also received a windfall from Restore Our State. They moved into an upscale retirement community in Raleigh. George baffled doctors and surprised everyone else but Lillian by surviving with reasonable vigor for two more years.

Lillian lived out a longer life in the home, to the delight of fellow residents and staff, with the possible exception of the cafeteria chef, whom she regularly scolded for overcooking her burgers.

***　　　　　　　***

***

Lew Perry took a job as city editor of the Yaupon Bay Advocate.

The Advocate's parent company struck an arrangement with Ames Colville for rookie reporters, one at a time, to spend a learning year at The Sand Dollar.

Ames tried going to church.

He didn't like it and quit.

***　　　　　　　***

***

Daniel Doar, Clyde Hunter and the goon were never seen again.

Chapter Forty-One

They had agreed to meet at Bitty and Beau's Coffee in Wilmington. Hood and Ames Colville were a bit early. They settled down with lattes and breakfast biscuits.

"Do I understand correctly?" Hood said. "The place is run by staff with intellectual and developmental disabilities?"

"Yes," Ames said. "It was founded by a couple with Down Syndrome in their family."

"Quite a story."

"Indeed."

Dolph Rea and Bethany Scott soon arrived hand in hand.

"Just coffee for us, please sir," Rea said to a young server with a radiant smile.

"How have you been?" Ames asked.

"We've been well," Rea said.

He eyed Hood.

"I guess it's time for us to make a decision."

"If you like."

"You'll give me a completely new identity?"

"Completely. You'll have a passport, a driver's license, an employment history, an extended family, even references. They are real people who will vouch for you if they're asked."

"And for this your fee is … ."

"Something you treasure but can do without."

"You'll simply demand what you want."

"Yes."

"You could demand a million dollars."

"That would be foolish of me. You don't have a million dollars."

"Payable in advance?"

"No. Only after I've given you the new identity."

"Suppose I renege."

"Then you'd have to live with knowing you'd broken your word."

"That's it?"

"That's it."

"This is very odd."

"It's the way I do business. I've never had a complaint."

Bethany Scott looked questions at Ames Colville.

"I've known him for years," Ames said. "He is a good man. He won't abuse your trust."

Rea turned to his fiancé. She tipped him the slightest nod.

"OK," he said to Hood. "I accept. How long before I get my new self?"

"Here it is," Hood said, passing a manila envelope across the table.

Rea and Bethany Scott rejoined their hands. He heaved a deep breath in and out.

"OK. What's the fee?"

"I want four years of your life."

"What?"

"I want you to pursue a higher education. You have a good mind and a gift for communication. You could be a valuable member of any community you chose to live in."

"I can't afford four years of school."

"I will pay. Wherever you choose to go."

"That's it?"

"Yes."

"You're serious?"

"Yes."

Bethany Scott dabbed away a tear.

The young server arrived with two coffees.

"I guess we'll have a couple of breakfast biscuits after all," Rea said.

"Yes, sir," the server said. "You bet."

Chapter Forty-Two

Billy Wakefield's Mom was in the church kitchen, arranging flowers for the Sunday service. Billy took advantage of the opportunity to get some library time.

He flopped the big Bible open and read the words out loud. They still sounded special, like they had been written by someone who had a lot of wisdom in his head and a bit of music, too. But they didn't pull at him the way they sometimes did, because he was focused on some thinking (Dad called it heavy lifting.)

He decided it didn't make sense to assume that bad things would only happen *in the abstract,* which was another way of saying they would only happen to other people. But while Father Pete's explanations of all that sounded OK when he gave them, sometimes they didn't seem completely helpful when you were out of church and actually dealing with stuff. Billy figured that growing up would be a lot more complicated than learning to tie a necktie and to josh with other men instead of saying right out what you really felt.

He decided he'd go over to church, where the air was always cool and quiet, and the sunlight through the windows made patterns on the floor and pews.

There he found Peter Llewellyn sitting by himself and staring up at the high cross behind the altar. Billy slipped in beside him.

"Father Pete?"

"Yes, Billy," Peter Llewellyn said without lowering his gaze.

"Can I ask you a question?"

"Sure."

"The other time, when we came home from vacation and you were helping keep those bad men from getting us?"

"Yes?"

"It looked like you wanted to hurt that man."

"Yes, Billy. I wanted very much to hurt him."

Something in Llewellyn's voice made Billy take a closer look. He saw the tracks of tears.

"Are you OK, Father Pete?"

"I don't know, Billy. I don't know."

Billy Wakefield took Peter Llewellyn's hand in his and held it for a long time.

THE END

.